Follow Mr. Stink's other adventures in:

The Stink Files, Dossier 001:
The Postman Always Brings Mice

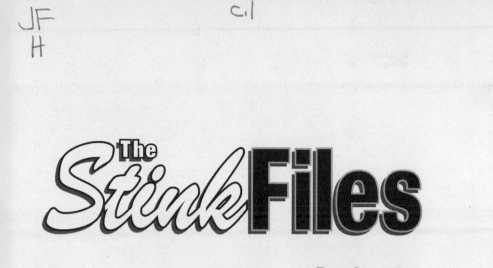

The StinkFiles

Dossier 002:
TO SCRATCH A THIEF

A Novel by **Holm & Hamel**

Illustrated by Brad Weinman

HarperCollinsPublishers

The Stink Files, Dossier 002: To Scratch a Thief

Text copyright © 2004 by Jennifer L. Holm and Jonathan Hamel

Illustrations copyright © 2004 by Brad Weinman

Printed in the United States of America. For information address HarperCollins Children's Books, a division of HarperCollins Publishers, 1350 Avenue of the Americas, New York, NY 10019.

www.harperchildrens.com

Library of Congress Cataloging-in-Publication Data

Holm & Hamel.

To scratch a thief / by Holm & Hamel ; illustrated by Brad Weinman.— 1st ed.

p.   cm. — (The Stink files ; dossier 002)

Summary: An enemy from Mr. Stink's past is targeting his new suburban family, and the international cat of mystery must discover the identity of his nemesis and defeat him.

ISBN 0-06-052982-2—ISBN 0-06-052983-0 (lib. bdg.)

[1. Cats—Fiction. 2. Spies—Fiction. 3. Mystery and detective stories.] I. Weinman, Brad, ill. II. Title.

PZ7.H732226To 2004

[Fic]—dc22   2003024281

CIP

AC

Typography by Karin Paprocki

1 2 3 4 5 6 7 8 9 10

❖

First Edition

To the real Bella, the loveliest calico I ever met.

—James

Dossier Contents

I WAS CREEPING through the ducts of the Palace Hotel.

It was dusty and dark, and the scent of the cat I had been following was growing faint. I paused and listened to my quarry's pawsteps echoing in the distance.

Then the sounds stopped.

I held my breath and crept forward, thankful as the way ahead grew brighter. A panel in the side of the duct sent horizontal slashes of light spilling across the way.

Then I saw him, crouched, as if he were lying in wait for me. But his back was turned: he was facing the wrong way! I couldn't believe my good fortune.

I stole closer in perfect silence, and then I pounced. I was in midair when his head snapped around and our eyes locked.

"Happy landings," he said. And laughed.

My paw landed on his tail, but the rest of me kept going.

I was falling into a hole. It was a trap!

The cat's mocking voice echoed from above. "And now . . . say good-bye, James."

I landed on a metal grate several feet below and looked up. Before I could gather my feet under me, I saw his paw reach out and flip a switch. The grate beneath me opened to reveal a deep shaft. And at the bottom: an immense whirring fan with deadly blades!

I flung my legs out, but my claws scrabbled uselessly against the slick metal sides of the shaft.

In a few seconds, I would be shredded. Pureed, even. Ground pâté of cat.

To think this had all started with cat food.

1

I Smell a Rat

THE CHIRPING of birds heralded the dawning of a new day in Woodland Park, New Jersey.

I sprang instantly alert and glanced out the window. The sky was still dark. Good. Plenty of time to get to the rendezvous point.

I jumped down from my fleece-lined bed and paused to make sure that my boy, Aaron, was still asleep. He was. The soft snoring coming from beneath the duvet proved just that.

Swift and silent as quicksilver I ran down the stairs and out the cat door in the back. I had practiced this exercise many times to make sure I had the timing down just right.

Nine seconds.

It was a warm spring morning. The patchy grass on the front lawn was moist with dew, and a light fog hung in the air. Perhaps we would have a lovely English-style rain later today, I thought hopefully. But I spared the weather no more thought as I ran down the block and past Bruno's house.

Thirty-seven seconds.

Right on time: a large green truck was lifting the Dumpster behind the gas station in its two big hydraulic arms. I dashed across the street, still deserted at this hour, and leaped undetected onto one of the arms, hitching an easy ride to the top of the truck. The trash was dumped and the Dumpster set back down.

Sixty-eight seconds on the whisker.

With a shudder and a hiss, the truck pulled out of the gas station and turned east, carrying me with it as an invisible stowaway.

Precisely according to plan.

Riding a garbage truck was hardly my idea of traveling in style. Indeed, my previous human, Sir Archibald, had always chauffeured me around in his collection of classic Jaguars.

I could still remember the first time I laid eyes on him.

I was just a kitten, living on a cat farm in the south of France, when one day a British spy named Archibald Ash pulled up in a red Jaguar C-Type. He was looking for the perfect cat to provide a cover story for his current mission: pursuing a nuclear arms smuggler whose hobby was breeding showcats.

After more than a year, we caught up to the smuggler on his yacht off the coast of Monte Carlo. When Sir Archibald and I stormed the boat, only one of his cats escaped, although it was his favorite, a Persian named Macavity. No accounting for taste: the fluffy white cat was polydactyl—that is, six-toed—and could only show in the Household Pet category. But all the important showcats in his collection were taken into custody, and the smuggler himself was sent to pay for his crimes. Sir Archibald and I always got our mark.

Sir Archibald had been the Director of a top-secret counterspy agency in England, an organization so secret that I'm afraid I may not even reveal its true name. For convenience, we shall call it simply MI9. I had learned much about the business of espionage during my years with Sir Archibald, but I had not learned enough to save his life. He had been poisoned, and I was now an ocean away from my former home in London.

In the last two months, I had made contact with a source who had traced the shortbread biscuits that had killed him. Imported from Norway, the biscuits had entered England through the port of Liverpool. (The very name made my mouth water.) Now I was eagerly awaiting the results of my transatlantic inquiries.

The garbage truck's route took it past the docks on its way to the Woodland Park dump. From my perch on top of it, I could see several tugboats nudging a massive cargo ship into position.

At the next stoplight, I leaped down from the truck and found a cat-sized hole in the electrified fence around Pier 94. By now, the ship had been secured, and a steady stream of rats was creeping down the cables, balancing with perfect skill in the dim light. One by one, they jumped to the pier and disappeared among the containers.

A sleek gray head appeared around a nearby corner. "Oy, beau'iful night for a ride in a Jaguar, eh?"

And I replied, "I prefer rainy afternoons."

This, of course, was the proper sign and countersign.

The rat hunkered down beside me and said in his thick, low-class accent, "Right, you must be Stink, then. I wasn't sure, you know: I didn't smell anything." He grinned, showing off a wicked set of crooked yellow fangs.

I growled. Everyone, it seemed, had a joke about the moniker my new family had given me. But it wasn't worth bothering to explain things to a rat who smelled strongly of bilge.

"The name is Bristlefur, James Edward Bristlefur. No time for chitchat, rat," I said sharply. "Do you have the information?"

He looked around furtively. "If you're ready with your end of the bargain, guv'nor."

I nodded and gave him directions to a nearby land-fill guarded by dogs with whom I had a good relation-ship—cousins of Bruno, the dog from my block. "The password is 'postman.' But one visit is all you and your friends get."

"Lovely." The rat rubbed his front paws together eagerly. "Righty-o. The warehouse you inquired about was completely deserted. Looked like it been that way for a long time. D'you want me mates to keep the place pegged?"

Wharf rats were excellent sources for information

about the international scene, but they generally lacked discretion. "Yes, but we can't risk being seen together again," I told him. "If you discover anything further, use the dead drop behind the Dumpster at Parkside Pet Foods."

A dead drop is a hidden location where messages are not likely to be disturbed, such as a hollow tree or an empty soda can, a common trick used by spies and counterspies. "Same terms, *if* you bring me something I can use."

I turned to go.

"Crikey, you just reminded me," the rat called after me. "Me mates did find an empty biscuit tin in the rubbish out back."

I stopped. "A biscuit tin? What kind?"

"Shortbread. From Norway. Just like you thought, guv."

I thanked the rat and stalked off. All this proved was that Sir Archibald's killer was still several steps ahead of me. The only clues I had found were ones he wanted me to find, it seemed: a set of altered baggage tags on my cat carrier and a white whisker on my boy's pillow. This biscuit tin was no different. What I needed was a solid lead.

But it would have to wait.

2

Breakfast at the Greens'

CAUGHT A passing garbage truck back to #9 North Tenth Avenue.

It stopped a block away from my family's house, and I leaped off, running down the street, through the cat door, and up the stairs, just in time to hear a steady beeping sound. The alarm was ringing, but my boy was still hunkered under his duvet, only a tuft of hair hinting he was there.

Typical.

I walked across his bedside table, turned off the alarm with my front paw, and stood on his head.

"Aw c'mon. Five more minutes," Aaron groaned.

I meowed, but he dislodged me and stuck his

into my speech lately. I made a mental note to watch myself, lest I lose the last ounce of my excellent breeding while living with this charming—but woefully ordinary—American family.

Sitting at the breakfast table and half covered in jam was Lily, Aaron's six-year-old little sister. Just the other day she had purposely dropped a gob of jam on me, to see what would happen.

The child saw me standing in the doorway, and her eyes brightened.

"Mom! Can I bring Mr. Stink to school for show-and-share?" she asked, a tinge of whine to her voice.

I shuddered at the thought of having to perform for a room of thirty first-graders. Little children adore pulling the tails of cats.

"No, Lily. Mr. Stink is not a toy," the mother said, much to my relief.

Aaron clomped heavily down the stairs and went over to the counter, where he fixed a bowl of cold cereal for himself and a bowl of the latest cat food for me.

"Here ya go, Stink," Aaron said, giving me a rough pat on the head before settling down to his own breakfast.

I sniffed the bowl tentatively. As a British cat, I was

head under a pillow.

A moment later, his mother appeared at the door. "You'd better listen to Mr. Stink, Aaron; otherwise you're going to miss the bus."

"Sounds good to me. Then I won't have to take that stupid math test," Aaron grumbled. I meowed louder, and he flung the covers back and sat up. "Okay, okay, I'm up." He sniffed. "Ew. You smell like garbage, Mr. Stink."

While I wouldn't have minded a bath myself, it was more important that Aaron have one. I waited until I heard water running in the bathroom, a sure sign my boy was fully awake, and headed downstairs for a quick tour of the house. One of my raggedy nails snagged on the carpet and I nearly fell down the stairs.

My claws were in dreadful shape. I couldn't help but think that Sir Archibald would have been disappointed in me. He was very insistent that a good counterspy always keep in the best of condition.

But there was no helping it. Ever since the Couch Incident, my boy's mother went ballistic if I so much as flexed my claws, even though another cat had done the damage. Or, I should say, she got well and truly cheesed off, as we used to say in London.

I had noticed quite a few Americanisms creeping

used to a hearty breakfast of fried kippers. Breakfast was a very different kettle of fish here in America. Aaron's father, Mr. Green, owned a pet supply store called Parkside Pet Foods. He liked to try out all the new varieties of cat food on me, and this latest batch was a macrobiotic soy blend called Karmic Kitty, whose label enthused, "For All the Lives of Your Cat." It was apparently produced by a commune of hippies somewhere in Taos, New Mexico.

The only decent food Mr. Green had brought home so far was a brand from France called Le Chat Gourmet. Le Chat Gourmet was delicious, a symphony of delicately prepared premium ingredients. You had to admire the French. They might be rude, but they certainly knew how to cook.

I would not even have touched the hippie concoction were it not my family duty to do so. I stuck my nose into the bowl and took a deep sniff to savor the bouquet. The vintage had a rich, earthy aroma. Very interesting. Another sniff revealed wood-chip undertones and a hint of pork. Quite promising, in fact.

One bite was enough, though. Earthy was an understatement. Karmic Kitty tasted like ground-up worms. I couldn't help myself: I spat it back into the bowl and took a drink of water to clear my palate.

"I guess hippies shouldn't be making cat food," Aaron's mother observed wryly. She was darting about the room in her usual fashion, piling papers into a briefcase.

My bowl vanished, and a fresh bowl of Le Chat Gourmet appeared in its place. My boy knew me well.

"Hey, where's Dad?" Aaron asked.

"Mm? Oh, he went out early to pick up some flyers from the copy shop," Mrs. Green said.

"What?" Aaron dropped his cereal spoon with a clatter. "But I need to talk to him about my project, remember?"

"I'm sorry, Aaron, I forgot. What project was this again?"

"The science fair," he said, exasperated. "You've been telling me all week to talk to Dad, and every night he's been coming home after I go to bed."

I had noticed that Mr. Green had been unusually busy, as a matter of fact.

"You know he was up late last night writing that essay for the Le Chat Gourmet contest," Mrs. Green said.

"But we're supposed to put the title on the sign-up sheet today, and I don't even know what we're doing!"

Aaron's mom stopped digging through her briefcase

and narrowed her eyes. "Weren't you supposed to start this project weeks ago?"

Aaron looked down guiltily. "Yeah, but I wanted Dad to, you know, help us come up with something cool that would win."

She made an exasperated noise. "Well, at this point I think passing is more important than winning, don't you? Do you have any ideas at all?"

"I don't know. Robby wants to do an ant farm."

"What's wrong with that?"

"Nothing, I guess."

"So do the ant farm. I'm sure it'll be fine."

"Okay," Aaron said. "Robby's mom really hates ants, though. Can we keep them here?"

Mrs. Green grimaced. "Just so long as the ants stay *in* the farm. The last thing we need is an ant infestation in this house. Now hurry up, you two, or you're going to miss the bus."

"Thanks, Mom," Aaron said, grabbing his lunch bag.

The morning fog had burned off, and it was shaping up to be a beautiful day. I walked with Aaron and Lily to the bus stop as was my habit. This had begun as a way of keeping my eye on a particularly cruel bully who had been intent on torturing Aaron. No one messed with my boy these days.

"Hey, Aaron," said Aaron's friend Robby, joining us on the walk. "What did your dad say?"

"Nothing. He wasn't home again. But Mom okayed the ant farm."

"Awesome!" Robby said. " 'Cause guess what? I already bought 'em. I've been hiding them in the garage."

Aaron gave Robby a funny look. "What is it with you and ants?"

Robby shrugged. "They're just cool."

"Geek."

"Dweeb."

They grinned at each other. And then there was no more time to talk because the bus pulled up.

"See ya later, Mr. Stink," Aaron said.

I watched Aaron get safely on the bus and headed back home.

3

The Thief Has Taste

I **WAS JUST** slipping through the cat door when I heard Mr. Green's MGB roar into the driveway. A few moments later, he ambled into the kitchen.

"There you are, Mr. Stink," Mr. Green said with a grin. "I've got a surprise for you."

Lately he had been bringing me toys. Toys! As if I were a kitten.

He drew one hand from behind his back and tossed a very fake stuffed mouse onto the floor in front of me. I looked at the gray rabbit fur, unimpressed.

"It's a SuperMouse 99," he said. "Still in product testing. It's supposed to be 'irresistible to cats of all ages.' What do you think?"

The thing smelled strongly of catnip, a vice I despise, but its tail had a small bell on it. I pounced on the mouse and ripped the tail off.

Mr. Green sighed heavily. "So much for that."

On the contrary, the bell would be an ideal early warning system for perimeter defense. I ran upstairs to leave it in my bed for later and returned to the kitchen, where Mr. Green was waiting for me.

"Ready to go to work?"

Mr. Green liked it when I accompanied him to Parkside Pet Foods during the day. He said I was good for business. As a Bengal cat in the prime of my life, I certainly was a handsome specimen. Or so the ladies told me when they came to the store.

Mr. Green held open the passenger side door of his car, and I hopped in and sat in my usual place on the seat. While the MGB was not as sleek as the cars in Sir Archibald's collection of Jaguars, I had grown rather fond of the tomato-red 1972 convertible with its cranky carburetor and torn upholstery.

As we passed Aaron's bus stop, I saw that Bruno was awake, chained in his yard as usual. He was an immense, ferocious-looking Shepherd-Rottweiler mutt who lived in the house adjacent to the bus stop.

Hey, Stink! Bruno barked to me. *If you throw a cat out a car window, do they call it kitty litter?*

Very funny, I meowed back.

Beside me, Mr. Green chuckled. "Anyone would think you two were carrying on a conversation."

As luck would have it, there was a Jaguar dealership that we usually passed on our way to Parkside Pet Foods. I stared longingly out the passenger window at the rows of gleaming high-performance machines.

"I know what you mean, Mr. Stink," Mr. Green said with a wistful sigh. "If things work out this week, maybe one day I'll be able to save up for one."

I puzzled at what he meant, but he said no more about it, and soon we had arrived at our destination.

Parkside Pet Foods had a cheerful green awning and a little electronic device on the door that played "How Much Is That Doggy in the Window?" whenever a customer entered. The store carried all manner of pet supplies: twenty-five brands of kitty litter, an impressive array of high-tech cat toys, a wall of rawhide chew bones, and more than thirty varieties of "gourmet" cat food, only one of which deserved the gourmet appellation.

While Mr. Green did not sell pets per se (cats and

dogs, that is), he did sell exotic fish and two hyper-active gerbils who spent all their time racing on a wheel. The gerbils were a bit wild-eyed, no doubt from hearing "How Much Is That Doggy . . ." over and over in a store that did not sell dogs. In fact, the innocent-looking rodents had terrible tempers and viciously bit anyone who picked them up. They had been bought and returned by no fewer than four families.

The creatures started squealing the moment Mr. Green's key entered the lock. My boy's father fed the animals first thing when he came into the store each morning, and there was always a feeding frenzy. Even the fish swam closer to the top of their tanks when the door opened.

Feed us now! We're staaarrrving! The gerbils squeaked loudly.

Mr. Green was humming to himself as he walked through the store, flicking on lights.

I jumped up onto the counter next to the cash register and stretched out in a pool of warm sun spilling from a skylight. By late morning, the patch would move to the floor, and I would take up my post in a very nice fleece-lined cat bed in the window. I was just settling down when I heard an enormous yelp.

It was Mr. Green!

I leaped off the counter and ran to the back store-room, where Mr. Green was staring in shock at an enormous pallet of cat food. Or rather, an enormous *empty* pallet.

For someone had ripped open the shipment and stolen all the food!

"I don't believe this," Mr. Green said, as he stared at the empty pallet in dismay.

I looked closely at the shipping label. It was Le Chat Gourmet.

Clearly, the thief, whoever he was, had good taste.

4

Word on the Street

AFTER SEVERAL hours, the police still had not shown up.

I paced back and forth in front of the entrance to the storeroom, eager to take another look, but thought it best not to disturb the evidence until after the detectives dusted for fingerprints. While we waited, Mr. Green spent his time on the phone.

"Of course I set the alarm! It was still armed when I arrived!" Mr. Green exclaimed in an exasperated voice. "Well, I don't know why! That's *your* job."

It was late afternoon by the time the police arrived. Judging from the long yellow smear of mustard on the front of the blue uniform of one and the green chunks of relish on the sleeve of the other, I surmised they had been busy responding to a crime at a local hot dog stand.

Americans.

"I'm positive I locked up when I went home last night. I'm very careful," Mr. Green insisted.

One cop was snapping photos of the empty pallet.

"Any sign of forced entry?" the shorter cop asked. His name tag read LIEUTENANT PETERSEN.

"No. The alarm didn't even go off."

"Was it set?"

"Of course!" Mr. Green cried. "I called the alarm company and they're sending someone out to look at it."

"Any cash missing?" the other cop asked. Mr. Green shook his head. "Anything valuable?"

"That was five hundred dollars' worth of cat food!" Mr. Green said. "Wholesale."

"Five hundred dollars?"

"It's gourmet," Mr. Green explained.

"What I meant was, is there anything else missing? Like maybe some exotic pet or something?" Lieutenant Petersen asked.

Mr. Green shook his head. "I sell mainly pet supplies."

The short cop was eyeing one of the aquariums. It featured a pair of angry-looking fish with sharp little teeth.

"You need a special license or something for those piranhas?" he asked.

"Well," Mr. Green began.

"Is it true they can strip a bone clean in five minutes?" Lieutenant Petersen asked.

"Look, do you have any ideas about who may have done this?" Mr. Green asked, his patience at an end. "Can't you take fingerprints or something?"

"We *could*, but . . . then we'd have to call in detectives and a forensics team and it makes a real mess," the cop said unenthusiastically, his eyes sliding over to me. I sat up a little straighter and looked him right back. "Are you sure your cat didn't do it?"

"It was an entire shipment! He'd explode if he ate that much food. Anyway, Mr. Stink is a good cat. He'd never do that," Mr. Green said.

"Mr. Stink, eh? I don't smell anything," the cop said with a snicker.

Humans always take everything so literally.

"Maybe the cat had a party, or something. He have any known associates, maybe a girlfriend acting suspiciously?" Petersen caught the other cop's eyes, and they both laughed.

"Look, Mr. Stink wasn't even here. I take him home with me every night and he's the only cat allowed in the store," Mr. Green said, completely aggravated now.

The cop flipped his pad shut. "Well, let us know if you find anything else missing. We'll make a few calls. Check the hospitals. See if any cats were brought in for overeating." He guffawed.

As Mr. Green escorted the two policemen to the front of the store, I heard one of them ask, "My wife has this toy poodle who's got really bad breath. Got anything for that?"

Clearly, the long arm of the law did not extend very far in Woodland Park, if these two were representative of the local crime-fighting force.

I padded to the storeroom to survey the crime scene myself.

The storeroom was a windowless area in the rear of Parkside Pet Foods with rows of shelves and a back entrance through which suppliers made their deliveries from a loading dock. This was usually done first thing Monday morning, after which Mr. Green closed the door and set the alarm.

Somehow, the thief had managed to bypass the alarm.

I sniffed around the empty case, hoping to learn something from the thief's scent. I had honed my natural ability at smell profiling, and I could generally deduce quite a bit from the scent left by criminals. But nowhere could I detect the smell of any strange humans in the storeroom.

However, I did smell a . . . *cat*? The scent was strange, hard to pin down. Yes, it was a cat, and a very unusual one at that. He was both young and old. Large and small. Uniformly unhealthy. Ranging in age from . . . from two to twelve! It didn't make any sense. Perhaps the thief had disguised his scent somehow, a bit of tradecraft I had used myself on occasion. But if the thief was a cat, how exactly did he get out with all that food? And without setting off the alarm?

I nosed along the wall below the alarm panel, looking for more clues. It didn't take long. The alarm wires had been chewed through and pushed together, creating a short circuit that had allowed the thief to act with impunity. I looked more closely. The tooth marks on the insulation were not those of rodents (the usual suspects in such a situation).

They were *cat* tooth marks!

It was time to speak to my operatives.

If there were two creatures who could sniff out missing food, it was Frankie and Vinnie—small-time street mice who turned a tidy profit in the Woodland Park food racket. Sir Archibald had always counseled his agents on the importance of developing their own network of reliable informants, and I was trying to follow his advice here in America. I waited for the two mice to show up for their daily report at the loading dock of Parkside Pet Foods.

"Dere was a plattah a' spilled cheese ovah at da deli on Thoid, but dat's about it, boss," Frankie squeaked.

"And it was some pretty good cheese, too," Vinnie added, licking his lips. "Smoked mozzarella! My favorite!"

The two mice had briefly moved to Staten Island after our first partnership but had returned after only a few weeks.

"Dat neighborhood's all locked up!" they had said. "You gotta know somebody who knows somebody just to get near one of doze big houses, and we ain't got doze kinda connections!"

Now, as they stood before me, I explained to them about the theft the night before.

"Le Chat Gourmet? Dat's da good stuff, ain't it?" Frankie asked. He bounded off to investigate.

I flicked my tail impatiently. "Have you heard any news of it?"

"Nah," Vinnie said. "A whole shipment? We'd a' heard about dat much stuff movin' on da street! Aside from dat cheese plattah, everyting's been real quiet from here to da storm drain on Tenth Avenue."

Frankie's voice echoed from underneath the empty pallet. "Not a crumb. It does sorta smell like a cat's been in here, but where'd all da bags go? It ain't like cats drive trucks." His pink nose poked back out.

I looked from one mouse to the other.

"I'm going to need a volunteer to stay here tonight and see if the thieves return. Frankie! Stop that!"

Frankie had wandered into a corner and was sniffing at an open tray of rat poison Mr. Green had set out to protect his stock.

"What?" he asked.

"That's rat poison, Frankie."

"But it smells so good!" he whined.

"That's the point, Frankie. Leave it alone," I ordered.

"Time to go, Mr. Stink," Mr. Green called.

"What about dem gerbils? Why can't dey watch da place?" Frankie asked.

"Because they can't get out of their cage," I said slowly. "Vinnie, you explain it to your cousin."

"Sure," Vinnie snickered, "I'll learn him all right."

I turned to go, calling over my shoulder, "Oh, and by the way, I happen to know that the bag of gerbil food is untied. Help yourselves, but DON'T EAT IT ALL!" I warned.

They high-fived each other.

As I bounded toward the front of the store, I heard Frankie say, "Cheese, I still can't believe we're working for a cat."

Mr. Green and I strolled out to the parking lot. He opened the door for me, and I growled low in my throat.

"What is it, Mr. Stink?" he asked.

There on the seat was another white whisker, identical to the calling card that had been left on my boy's pillow several months ago. That could mean only one thing.

Some cat wanted me to know that this theft was no random crime. This was the work of the same cat who had threatened my boy, who had almost gotten me declawed, and who had engineered to have me misdirected here to New Jersey.

The same cat who had murdered Sir Archibald.

5

A Sticky Situation

SO THE police have no leads?" Mrs. Green asked
at the supper table that night. "Maybe it was a
bunch of kids or something. Like a prank."

"I just have a hard time believing it was a group of
teenagers," Mr. Green said, sounding glum. "I guess
the only thing I can do is file a claim with the insur-
ance company."

I sat on the ledge of the bay window behind the
dinner table and looked out at the family's backyard,
puzzling over my own leads. Who was this cat who
was after my family? I had made more than my share
of enemies in my time as an unofficial MI9 operative.
Whoever it was, the absence of any hard evidence

marked him as a professional. Perhaps I should not have left amateurs like Frankie and Vinnie to keep watch at the store. I decided to check on them after dinner.

"It's just so frustrating," Mr. Green was saying. "After all the work I've been doing to get ready for this week. We could have been set for the rest of the year."

"I know, honey," his wife said. "It'll work out."

"I know what you can do, Dad!" Aaron said in an excited voice. "You could get one of those spy cameras. You know, it could be hidden and everything."

"Maybe," Mr. Green said with a tired expression. "We'll see what the alarm company says when they come."

I sniffed. Sir Archibald had always been dismissive of hidden surveillance cameras. He said any spy worth his salt could spot one in under a minute.

"Guess what, Dad?" Aaron said. "Robby and me are doing an ant farm for the science fair."

"That's great, Aaron," Mr. Green said automatically. He yawned. "You know what, I think I'm just going to go to bed. I have to get up early tomorrow."

"Wait, can I show you the ant farm? I wanted to ask you for some advice." Aaron and Robby had moved the ant farm into Aaron's room that afternoon after school.

"I promise I'll look at it tomorrow," Aaron's father told him. He ruffled his son's hair.

"Can I look at the ant farm?" Lily whined.

"No, Lily, you'll mess it up," Aaron said. "Stay out of my room."

"You kids help your mom with the dishes," Mr. Green said, and then he walked out of the kitchen and upstairs.

Aaron sighed and looked down at his plate.

I waited until Aaron fell asleep, then slipped out of his room to do a quick sweep of the house. After all, I was responsible for the safety and well-being of my humans.

Since taking residence at #9 North Tenth Avenue, I had established a protocol to keep tabs on any intruders. For instance, I had closed up a crawlspace in the basement that had previously been used by mice. And at several other points of entry (animal entry, that is) throughout the house, I had set booby traps.

Everything seemed to be in good order. Satisfied, I went to my cat door and carefully placed a long whisker across the entrance and licked it until it stuck there. It was an old spy trick. If the whisker was moved, then I would know that someone besides myself had gone through the door.

I looked at my work with satisfaction and headed out into the night.

It was a cool, clear spring night with just a touch of moisture in the air. As I walked down the sidewalks, I was reminded of all my midnight patrols in London. Sometimes it seemed so long ago.

"Thought I smelled something," I heard a voice say. "How ya doin', Stink?"

I looked up to see Bruno resting on his paws in front of his house. Bruno's human used to bully Aaron, but the dog and I maintained a cordial relationship.

"There's been a theft at the pet food store," I said. "Someone stole an entire shipment of Le Chat Gourmet."

He raised his eyebrows. "Gee, I wonder who would be stealing food?"

Bruno was referring to Kitty, a local street cat, who was partial to stealing food from other pets' dishes. She had, in fact, stolen food from both Bruno and myself.

"No, it was the work of a professional," I told

Bruno. "Someone with far more experience than our friend Kitty." And intelligence, I might have added, but there was no need to be rude.

Bruno nodded. "Probably was that brother of hers, Bugs. Trust me, he didn't get that fat living on the street."

"I'll keep it in mind, but I have other pressing business at the moment."

"Well if you do see Kitty, tell her I've decided I like cats after all, but I still don't think I could eat a whole one." Bruno grinned, revealing sharp teeth.

"Very funny. Where do you get all your jokes?"

Bruno stretched. "I get 'em on the Bark Network."

"The Bark Network?"

"Yeah, you don't have that in England? Dogs bark and pass messages long distance that way. It's s'posed to be for emergencies, but lately everybody just sends jokes and stuff."

Interesting. In England, the dogs called it the Bark Exchange. "I have one for you, Bruno: what has four legs and an arm?"

"What?"

"A happy Rottweiler."

The dog grinned devilishly and licked his chops. "I'll pass that one on."

"See you later, Bruno," I said.

"Not if I smell you first," Bruno replied.

I rolled my eyes and shook my head.

Parkside Pet Foods was dark except for the lights from the fish tanks. From out front all seemed quiet. Then I heard the terrified squeaking.

"Help! Help!" Frankie and Vinnie were screaming at the top of their mouse lungs.

I raced around to the back of the store. The door was shut, but I could still hear their voices clearly. They seemed to be coming from the roof! I jumped onto the Dumpster, and from there onto the gravel-strewn roof. The skylight over the showroom had been forced open just wide enough for a cat to get through!

I squeezed in and jumped down onto the top shelf of an aquarium rack.

"Help!" Vinnie squeaked desperately.

Below me, I could see the two mice, their feet stuck in glue traps, dangling over the piranha tank!

The piranhas were circling the surface of the water like hungry sharks. The glue traps were precariously balanced on the edge of the tank, baited with bits of cheese. No doubt Frankie and Vinnie's stomachs had

gotten them into this mess.

"Boss! Help us!" Frankie squeaked hoarsely.

Just then, my sharp ears detected movement in the back storeroom.

The thief was still here! But not for long by the sound of things. I could catch him if only—

"We're gonna be fish food!" Frankie squeaked.

I looked between the storeroom and the two mice, my heart racing.

6

Cat with a Past

I WAS FROZEN.

The thief was on his way out the back door. Immediately below me, Frankie and Vinnie were dangling above a tank of very hungry-looking piranhas.

"What're you waitin' for?" Vinnie squeaked.

Then Frankie screamed in pain! "It got my tail, it got my tail! Owwwww . . ."

The thief would have to wait for another day, I thought with a wistful glance at the storeroom. In three great leaps, I bounded from one rack of shelves to the other, and down until I was on the shelf next to the piranha tank. Grasping Frankie gently in my mouth, I carried him down to the floor, trap and all.

Then I did the same for Vinnie.

"Wait here," I told them as I ran into the back room.

"Where you think we're goin' anyway?" Vinnie snapped irritably, trying to extricate his feet from the glue trap.

But I was too late. The storeroom was empty, and the door to the loading dock was just swinging shut. I ran out the door and into the dark night, but there was no sight of him. He was gone.

And so was the Karmic Kitty. All of it.

"Ow! Be careful!" Vinnie squeaked loudly as I tried to pull his tail out of the glue trap. I had managed to get all of his feet out, but his tail was still stuck.

"At least you have a tail," Frankie moaned. He was licking at the stubby length of tail he still had left. One of the piranhas had actually leaped out of the water and bitten it in half.

"You can always grow another one," Vinnie said.

Frankie perked up. "I can?"

"No, Frankie, you can't." I sighed. We would be here all night at this rate. I tried another tactic. "Say, Vinnie, look at that piece of cheese over there."

"Where?" he asked, sniffing eagerly.

While his head was turned, I grabbed him in my

mouth and yanked him off the glue trap. He came free with an enormous yelp.

"Ouch!" the mouse said, rubbing his tail. "Look what you did! I'm bald!"

There was a long strip of gray fur still resting on the glue trap.

"Dis is what we get working for a cat," Frankie muttered.

"Now, can we go over what happened tonight?" I asked.

The two mice eyed each other warily.

"See, we was just—" Vinnie said.

"Dere was dis cheese sitting on the shelf and—" Frankie said simultaneously.

"Shut up, Frankie!" Vinnie said, smacking him.

"You shut up! I'm da injured party here!"

I rolled my eyes. Perhaps I needed to rethink the caliber of my informants.

"Enough!" I growled. "Someone obviously set a trap for you. And that someone also intended for you to become the piranhas' supper."

Both mice gulped.

"So I think it is important that you share with me any possible clues as to the identity of the perpetrator."

The two mice blinked at that.

Finally, Vinnie spoke. "Look, we was doing what you told us, you know, patrollin' da back storeroom and stuff, when all of a sudden we smelled dat cheese. So we came out here to get a look and . . . bam! We're stuck like rats in a trap."

"While we was stuck, we heard a whole bunch of cats stealing da food in da back," Frankie whined. "We screamed for help, but dey just laughed."

Multiple cats. That explained the strange smell!

"Yeah," Vinnie said quickly. "Dey was definitely cats. Street cats by da smell of them."

"Local?" I asked.

"Hard to say," Vinnie said.

But who was the ringleader? Dogs might regularly run in packs, but it took a very strong personality to herd cats.

"Good. Is there anything else you can remember?" I prodded. A counterspy's greatest weapon was information.

"There was one other thing," Vinnie said finally.

"Go on," I urged.

Frankie piped up. "One of dem cats was really big, and had dis funny accent."

"Funny how?"

"Like he was a foreigner or somethin'," Vinnie said.

"And one a' his ears was torn up real bad," Frankie added.

Interesting.

The theft was discovered the next morning, a Saturday.

Mr. Green was beside himself. "They stole all the Karmic Kitty?" he exclaimed, looking at the empty pallet.

I wanted to tell him that the thieves got what they deserved. Perhaps I could just follow the most miserable-looking cats through town to find the culprits. So much for the thieves having good taste.

After placing a call to the police, who assured him they would be "right over," Mr. Green headed out to a discount store and returned with several large shopping bags. Naturally, the police had not been by. My boy, however, showed up on his bike after hearing the news.

"Wow, what's all that?" Aaron asked, looking at the pile on the counter. There were a bat, pepper spray, flashlights, duct tape, rope, several disposable cameras, and a brand-new sleeping bag in camouflage.

"I'm going to catch this thief myself," Mr. Green said in a determined voice. "I'm sleeping here tonight."

"Cool," Aaron said. "Can I sleep over, too? That way I can tie him up when you whack him over the head!"

Mr. Green shook his head. "Sorry, Aaron, it's too dangerous."

Aaron's face fell.

The phone rang and Mr. Green snatched it up. "Parkside Pet Foods."

"Dad, what if I—," Aaron began but Mr. Green held up a finger.

"What do you mean pet food's not covered under the policy? This is a pet food store!" Mr. Green said into the phone.

A man wearing a baseball hat that said CROOK STOPPERS ALARM COMPANY popped his head through the door of the storeroom. "I found your alarm problem. Looks like you got rats. Ate right through the wires. Normally, that'd set it off, but they shorted the wires together. It's the darndest thing I've ever seen."

The front door opened and "How Much Is That Doggy . . . " began playing loudly.

"Afternoon, Mr. Green," Lieutenant Petersen said. "So what got stolen this time? Kitty litter?" He chuckled.

"You want me to run the wire through some aluminum tubing?" the alarm repairman called out. "I got some in the truck."

Mr. Green gave a harassed-sounding sigh. "Do whatever you want! I don't know!"

"Dad!"

"Aaron, I don't have time now," Mr. Green said. He fumbled for his wallet. "Here's a couple of bucks. Bike over to the Happy Clown and get us some ice cream, okay?"

Then I heard a low whistle.

Check out the babe, the gerbils squeaked loudly.

I blinked twice in surprise.

For on the other side of the glass was a beautiful orange-furred cat with striking green eyes.

I felt my heart thump painfully in my chest.

She stared at me for a long moment and then darted away.

Isabella.

The past came rushing back like an unwanted hair-ball.

Isabella and I had met during one of Sir Archibald's missions in Switzerland. Even thinking of snowcapped mountains brought an ache to my throat.

Sir Archibald had been conducting a sting operation on a large diamond cartel smuggling illegal gems from Africa into Europe. We had taken temporary quarters above a café in a remote village in the Alps. It was there that I first met Isabella—that starry evening that changed my life forever.

My human and I were enjoying a well-deserved supper in the café. It had been a trying day, involving a high-speed chase along a winding mountain road. In the end, the diamond runner had eluded us.

I was sitting on a chair next to Sir Archibald as was my habit (pets in restaurants are much more acceptable in Europe than here in America) when she strolled by. Quite honestly, she was the most exquisite creature I had ever seen. Naturally, I decided to introduce myself to her.

"The name is Bristlefur, James Edward Bristlefur. At your service," I said gallantly.

"Isabella," she purred back with a slight Italian accent, blinking at me with her large green eyes. "My friends call me Bella. And I do hope we'll be friends." She wore a glittering diamond collar around her neck.

But ours was a doomed relationship. Too late I learned that her father was Don Catleone, one of the most ruthless leaders of organized crime the world over. In fact, the diamond thieves Sir Archibald and I were tracking were his current humans.

I could not spend my life with the daughter of an underworld boss, just as she could not spend hers with a British counterspy whose sworn duty was to bring down her father and his empire. I begged her to leave her father and a life of crime, but she refused. We parted tearfully, and I truly thought I'd never see her whiskers again—but here she was in Woodland Park.

The only question was: why?

7

A Lead

I SPENT THE rest of the day following up on leads.

My contacts at the Humane Society and at Sammy's Pet Store, two places where a foreign cat would not go unnoticed, assured me that there had been no new arrivals. There had been quite a number of kittens showing up around town, but that was to be expected as it was spring. It seemed I had hit a dead end. And then I remembered Bruno's taunt about Kitty. Street cats were territorial and were the first to know about any new cats in town.

I found Kitty in her usual haunt: the immense Dumpster behind the petrol station. She was banging around inside, making a tremendous racket.

I leaped on top and peered in. Her head was stuck in an empty jar of pickled herring. At least I didn't need to worry that *she* was the criminal mastermind.

"Good afternoon, Kitty," I drawled, looking down at her.

Kitty was so startled that she spun around, banging the jar against the side of the Dumpster with a metallic clang. She sat back, stunned.

"What do *you* want?" she asked, her voice muffled by the jar.

"You wouldn't happen to know anything about a theft at the pet food store, now, would you?"

A guilty look flicked across her face, but she shook her head quickly. Or tried to.

"I had nuttin' to do with it," she said defiantly.

"What about Bugs?"

"Ahh, Bugsy's back in the pound," she said. "Turned himself in last week."

"And the foreign gentleman with the torn ear who forced you to scratch up the sofa in my family's house? Have you seen him around lately?"

At this, she looked genuinely frightened. "I ain't seen him, and I don't want to!"

Kitty was proving to be a dead end.

"Very well," I said. I turned to go.

"Hey!" Kitty shouted. "Ain't ya gonna help me get this jar off my head?"

I looked into the distance. "Well, look who it is— Bruno!"

Kitty yelped and spun around, banging her head against the side of the Dumpster again, harder. The glass shattered.

"There, I helped you," I said. "But don't go anywhere. I might have some more questions for you."

"Where would I go? I ain't got nuttin' better to do," she said.

I had an idea.

"Kitty," I said with a smile. "Would you like a job?"

Aaron and Robby were hard at work on their science fair project when I returned home.

The ant farm was simple: two pieces of glass framed with a lid and a quantity of dirt pressed between them. And, of course, a host of tiny black ants running around. I wasn't quite sure why ants in dirt were considered a scientific achievement, but so long as my boy was happy, that was fine with me.

"There you are, Mr. Stink," Aaron said, looking up from the floor of his bedroom. He and Robby were spread out on a plastic tarp constructing a large-scale papier-mâché model of a soldier ant. "I put your food out downstairs."

I rubbed up against my boy to show I was pleased with him.

"Did you hear about what happened to Mr. Whipple's class during science yesterday?" Aaron asked.

Robby's eyes widened. "No, but I saw everyone run out of the classroom."

"Jack told me Mr. Whipple had this huge cooler of dry ice in the sink for some experiment, and Kyle thought it would be funny to test it out, so he turned on the hot water full blast when Mr. Whipple's back was turned. Next thing you know, it totally fogged up the place! I heard he got detention for like a month! Guess we don't have to worry about him on the bus after school for a while."

"I would've paid to see the look on his face," Robby said. He was tearing a sheet of newspaper into long, thin strips.

"Me, too," Aaron said with a chuckle. "So I heard we're dissecting worms this week."

"Cool," Robby said.

The boys' project was nearing completion, and I had to admit it was very impressive. In addition to the ant farm, there was a full-color backdrop with diagrams of the different kinds of ants and tunnels. The papier-mâché ant would be the crowning glory.

"I think this should do it," Robby said. "We can paint it after it dries, and label it and stuff."

"Wait till my dad sees this," Aaron said admiringly.

"You're so lucky. My dad just cares about when I play sports. And usually only when I win."

Aaron was quiet for a moment, then said, "Hey. Did I tell you my dad and I are gonna sleep over tonight at the store to catch the thief? We're gonna knock him out with a baseball bat and tie him up with duct tape."

"No way! Your dad is so cool! My dad would never let me do that," Robby said.

Aaron's smile was strained. "Yeah, he sure is."

Something caught my eye. There, on the floor, was today's newspaper, which they had been using for the papier-mâché. The headline screamed:

INTERNATIONAL CAT SHOW IN TOWN

The article went on to say:

> The Palace Hotel will play host to the esteemed show. Over a thousand cats representing more than thirty countries worldwide will be in attendance. . . .

Finally, a lead!

8

Assaulted by a Refrigerator

MR. GREEN spent an extremely uncomfortable and completely uneventful night on the floor of Parkside Pet Foods. The thieves did not show up.

While the family sat down to breakfast, I headed to the Palace Hotel in downtown Woodland Park. There was a huge banner spread across the front announcing, "Welcome International Pet Show."

Part of my training as an operative was to blend seamlessly into any crowd. In this instance, I was a natural. I just sidled up to a harried-looking tourist and strolled along beside him into the lobby of the hotel as if he were my human.

It was chaos inside. Row after row of animal carriers packed with meowing cats crowded the room. These cats, I knew, were the best of the best—some of the most outstanding examples of their breed in the entire world. Still, for all their flawless pedigree, they didn't seem to have very good manners and were bickering like overpaid Hollywood stars.

Her cage is bigger than mine! I was promised the biggest cage! a Maine Coon Cat was shouting irritably.

Look at that Siamese! a Manx shouted indignantly. *She's wearing the same collar as me. I thought this was a one-of-a-kind collar!*

I need to use the litter box now! a Blue Russian meowed.

Well, take a look at her. She's gained a few ounces around the middle. Probably back on the all-cream diet! one catty Burmese murmured to another.

At the front desk, a human couple was arguing with the clerk. Their cat, a tiny, hairless creature with an enormous pink bow and a miserable expression, sat at their feet shaking. She looked as if she were freezing to death.

"I specifically said that we were to have two rooms with a connecting door," the woman was saying in a loud voice. "Princess needs her own room. Otherwise she gets very nervous before the show."

"I'm sorry, ma'am," the clerk said, "but we're all booked up. What if we brought in a roll-away bed for your animal?"

"She is not an animal," the woman hissed. "She is a prize-winning Sphynx! She has her own website, you know."

Everywhere I looked there were advertisements. One announced, "New Pet Fashions, the Viscount Ballroom," and another said, "Feng Shui for Your Cat, Crown Prince Hall." Still another said, "Feline Horoscopes, the Regency Room."

I wandered down the corridor and squeezed into the feline horoscope lecture hall.

A very large cat wearing a chenille scarf sat near the back accompanied by an equally large human wearing a matching scarf. The cat turned to me and said in a deep, throaty voice with a distinctly Texan accent, "What's *your* sign, honey?"

"Leo, of course," I said with a wink.

I looked around the room. Most of the cats in here seemed to be Americans. Time for a little Bristlefur charm. "You wouldn't happen to know where most of the international cats are right now?" I asked.

"Sure, honey, there's a grooming clinic going on in

the Lord Chamberlain Room. They're all in there. Those Europeans love their fashion. Apparently the hot new trend out of Italy is hats. Sounds awful if you ask me."

"Thank you," I said and sauntered out.

"Hope to see you later, sugar," she purred.

The elevator bell rang for the third floor, and I stepped out into the corridor, following the signs for the Lord Chamberlain Room. There, at the end of the hall, was a large, open room with row after row of cats sitting next to their owners, while up front a stylist was giving instructions on how to give your cat highlights.

The accents barraged my ears the minute I stepped through the door. There were representatives from every cat breed in the world here. I saw an Ocicat, an American Bobtail, a Balinese, a Devon Rex, a Scottish Fold, a Javanese, a Havana Brown, and even a Turkish Angora.

Bonjour! a French Chartreux meowed to me.

I roamed the rows of chairs, but it was completely useless. They *all* had foreign accents. I would never find the thief here. Why, it could be *any* one of them!

Suddenly, I caught a whiff of Le Chat Gourmet. I aimed my nose in the direction of the smell. Did I mention that I have an excellent nose? And my nose was telling me that the source of the smell was somewhere behind the stage. I caught a glimpse of a tail vanishing behind a curtain there.

I have you now, I thought.

I took off after the cat, bounding behind the curtain and into a dimly lit service corridor. The cat disappeared around a corner. The scent of Le Chat Gourmet was stronger, though, so I knew I had not imagined it. I ran faster, trying to catch up to the cat, and as I rounded the corner, I ran right into a—

Refrigerator.

I hit it so hard that I fell back onto the floor, stunned.

When I looked up, I saw that it wasn't a refrigerator at all. It was a cat, a Norwegian Forest Cat if I wasn't mistaken. He was tall and thick and neckless, and his right ear looked like someone had taken a bite out of it. This was no showcat, that much was clear.

"Excuse me, who are you?" I asked.

"Your vorst nightmare," the cat growled menacingly.

A huge paw descended, and I thought the building had collapsed on me. As blackness overcame me, I couldn't help but think that the Norwegian accent was familiar.

I was unconscious before I hit the floor.

9

A Beautiful Stranger

I WAS HAVING the most marvelous dream.

I was in Paris with Isabella. We were strolling down the Champs-Elysées. It was spring, and we were in love.

"James," Isabella purred, the sun catching in her fur. "Why don't we go to the Eiffel Tower?"

"As my lady wishes," I said with a smile.

I placed one foot into the boulevard and looked back to smile at Isabella. There was an expression of perfect horror on her face.

"Oh, James!" she gasped. "Look out!"

I looked up. A refrigerator was falling from the sky.

And then I heard a voice say, "Maybe we should try smelling salts or something."

I blinked one eye open to see several human ladies leaning over me. They were all wearing name tags for the cat show. The one closest to me had a tag that read, HI, MY NAME IS FLO.

"He's alive!" Flo said.

"Poor thing," said a woman wearing HI, MY NAME IS DOTTIE.

My head was pounding. What had happened? I rubbed a paw behind my ear and winced. Ow. It all came rushing back with painful, *very painful*, clarity.

The refrigerator cat.

"I wonder whose cat he is," Flo was saying. "He's definitely a showcat. Purebred Bengal by the looks of him."

I lifted up my head, and the women cooed at me. Did I mention that I have a way with the ladies?

"Quick, someone get him a bed," Flo ordered. "And have them make an announcement over the PA system."

Ah, Flo, what a lovely lady in spite of her . . . purple hair? Had the blow to my head somehow damaged my eyesight? I focused on the woman. No, she definitely had purple hair.

Another lady came rushing over with a padded bed, and I was gently lifted and placed on it.

"There ya go, darling," Flo said.

A moment later, a voice boomed. "If someone is missing a showcat, a Bengal showcat, please go to the Lord Chamberlain Room and pick up your cat. Thank you."

I wanted to say that my boy would pick me up if they would just kindly call the phone number on my tags. But when I absently scratched the collar on my neck, I discovered that it and my tags were . . . gone!

Then to my utter horror, Flo said sadly, "It's a shame his owner didn't give him any tags. If no one claims him, I guess we'll have to send him to the Humane Society."

I gasped (although I confess it sounded more as if I were bringing up a hairball). But really. The Humane Society? When I'd first arrived in America, I had been sent to the Humane Society, and I cannot imagine a worse fate than to go back to that place.

I eyed the ballroom desperately. The main entrance was wide open.

"He'll definitely get adopted there," someone was saying.

I nuzzled into Flo's hand, rubbing her.

"What a darling," she said, leaning her head down.

And then I leaped. Right over her purple hair. Or

should I say *with* her purple hair, for my aim was slightly off, no doubt from a mild concussion, and my back foot snagged the hair and dragged it down to the floor.

"Close the door! Close the door!" Flo shrieked. "He's got my wig!"

I kicked away the annoying wig and ran for the door, my heart pounding. Luck was my friend, for the small woman by the door hesitated when she saw twenty-five pounds of ferocious Bengal cat bearing down on her. I leaped past her and out the door. Behind me, the ladies gave chase.

"He's going down the hallway!"

The hotel corridors seemed to me a maze as I dodged pedestrians dragging luggage on wheels. The door to a stairwell was open and I slipped in, taking the stairs three at a time. Miraculously, I didn't hear anyone following me. I had given them the slip! I ran out the open door to the lobby. At that exact moment the elevator doors opened, and there were Flo and her herd.

"Guard! Stop that cat!" she shrieked at the top of her lungs to the sleepy-looking security guard at the front door.

Everyone in the lobby froze, staring at me as I ran

for the main entrance. But the security guard was apparently not as sleepy-looking as I thought, for he was already closing the glass doors.

I skidded to a halt mere steps away from him.

"Now, just be calm, cat," the guard said in a placating voice, advancing on me. "No one's gonna hurt you."

I turned tail, easily eluding his grasp, and ran back out of the lobby with him in hot pursuit.

I heard the guard pull out his radio and gasp, "I'm in pursuit of a cat. Striped. Dangerous. Might be rabid. He's headed toward the snack bar."

Flo shrieked, "He's not dangerous. He's a showcat. He's worth thousands of dollars. Don't hurt him!"

The security guard pulled out his radio once more. "Me again," he said. "The cat is not dangerous. Repeat. The cat is not dangerous. Do not use undue force."

Excuse me, but I was a trained counterspy. I was, in fact, *very* dangerous. Or rather, I would be if my claws were not so dull and I hadn't recently been beaten up by a refrigerator.

I ran fast, dodging an oncoming crowd of conference attendees and their cats. Far ahead of me I saw another blue-garbed figure. No doubt another security guard. Behind me I could hear the first guard cursing as he bumped into a room service cart. How was I going to get out of this? Suddenly, a paw beckoned me from inside the wall.

An exotic voice whispered, "Psst, this way."

A small grate on the bottom of the wall was open, and a gray cat with glittering green eyes stood just inside the opening.

"Follow me," the cat said, and I did.

I was led up through a rabbit warren of tunnels, the ductwork of the hotel. The cat ran quickly down the dark, narrow spaces. Finally, when it was clear that we were quite safe, my guide paused and faced me.

"I can't thank you enough," I said, panting.

"Up to your old tricks again, I see, James," the cat said, and reached up a paw and began to bathe his face. The gray fell away, revealing . . .

Orange fur!

I could hardly believe my eyes.

Isabella laughed. "A delight to see you again as well, James. Although . . . you could use a bath yourself." She winked and wiped a line of gray powder from my flank. "These ducts are dusty."

"Wait," I said, stilling her paw. I had an idea. "Do you know a way out of here?"

"Yes," she said, arching an eyebrow. "You have

something in mind?"

"Trust me," I said, my old confidence restored. Isabella was here! It could only mean she had left her father and a life of crime to be with me!

We slipped out of the tunnel, and soon we were back in the main lobby.

A new security guard spied us and said, "I've found the cat. Actually, two of them. Repeat. Two gray cats."

A staticky voice came over his radio.

"That's not him. The cat we're looking for is striped. A Bengal is what they're calling it. Kind of looks like a small tiger."

The guard eyed us suspiciously. "Roger that. What should I do with these two?"

"What do I care? There's hundreds of cats in the hotel this weekend. Let someone else deal with it. We're not animal control," the voice squawked back.

The guard grumbled, and Isabella and I sauntered out the front doors to freedom.

"Just like old times," I said affectionately, smiling at Isabella. "Me saving you, that is."

"Actually, *I* saved *you*," she replied saucily.

"Of course," I conceded. "What are you doing in Woodland Park?"

"I live here now, James," she said.

I paused on the sidewalk, just taking in the sight of her. Even covered in dust, she was beautiful.

"It is so good to see you, Bella," I said.

"Actually, James," she said, "my father sent me."

"Your father," I said dully. "I see."

So she hadn't left her family behind after all.

"Will you come with me?" she asked.

My heart hardened. "No," I said coldly.

And walked away.

10

An Offer I Can't Refuse

RETURNED HOME to hear Mrs. Green lecturing Aaron in a loud voice tinged with hysteria.

"Didn't I tell you to be very careful with those ants? Didn't I?" she demanded, shaking a can of ant spray at him.

"But Mom—" Aaron said miserably.

"I'm going to have to call in a professional exterminator, you know. There's hundreds of them! Probably all laying eggs!"

"Only the queens lay eggs," my boy muttered.

"Are you contradicting me, young man?" she said dangerously.

"But it's not my fault!"

Mrs. Green put her hands on her hips. "You expect me to believe that someone came into your room and let those ants out? Who exactly?"

Aaron squirmed. "Well, I don't know, maybe Lily did it. She always—"

"Lily's at gymnastics. You know that. Oh, just wait until your father gets home."

I didn't wait to hear any more. I padded quickly upstairs.

There were dead ants lying in the hall, no doubt victims of Mrs. Green's spray. But as I neared my boy's room, I saw frenetic little black ants everywhere on the carpet.

I ventured inside and inspected the farm, treading carefully to avoid the ants streaming out in all directions. The lid was slightly ajar, as if Aaron had carelessly left it that way. But I knew my boy. He would never have left the lid open—he cared too much about this project.

Someone had come into this room, *my boy's* room, and destroyed his project to get at me.

That someone had gone too far.

I could barely contain my fury. I roamed the house, flexing my claws, looking for something—anything—

to scratch. How was I supposed to protect my boy with my claws in the state they were in?

Mrs. Green saw me and said, "Oh no you don't. Out. I'll take you back to the pound before I let you ruin any more furniture." With that she unceremoniously kicked me out the front door.

My boy was already sitting on the front step, a despondent expression on his face. I went and sat next to him.

"You got kicked out, too, huh?" he asked me.

A moment later the MGB came screeching into the driveway. The door opened and Mr. Green emerged.

"Your mother called me at the store. You are in big trouble, young man," he said.

"But Dad—" Aaron said.

"No buts. This was the last thing I needed. You know how busy I am with the cat show in town!" He shot Aaron an aggravated look. "Now I have to go in and calm down your mother. I'm really disappointed in you, Aaron," Mr. Green said, and then walked through the door.

Aaron's face fell.

"The only time he pays attention to me is when I'm in trouble," my boy said in a hollow voice. "It's not fair, Mr. Stink."

It certainly wasn't, especially when he was completely blameless. I rubbed against his shoulder and purred.

"Knock it off," Aaron said, his face set in a determined frown, but I just purred louder. After a minute he rubbed me back.

"At least you still like me," he said, the ghost of a smile on his face.

Kitty strolled up a moment later, and I led her around to the back of the house.

"Reporting for duty, boss," she said. "I ain't never had a job before. How are you, like, gonna pay me?"

"My humans own a pet food store. I'm sure you can figure it out," I said dryly. "Now, your sole task is to guard this door. Let no one inside, understand?"

"You got it, boss. Whatever you say," she said, all confidence. Her smile slipped. "Uh, what do I do if someone tries to get in?"

"If they're too much for you, run down the block and tell Bruno." I could see her start to panic. "He won't eat you. I will inform him that you are working for me now."

Her nose wrinkled. "But he's chained up. What can he do?"

"He'll get a message to me through the Bark Network. And any nearby dogs may be able to run over and help," I explained. "Now I have to go."

After resetting the whisker on the cat door, I went straight over to Bruno's to relay the day's events. As we talked, I sharpened my claws on the skinny sapling next to his doghouse. But there was very little bark, and my claws just slid down it without getting any sharper.

"So who do you think is behind it?" he asked.

I thought about Isabella's invitation to meet with her father.

"It has to be Don Catleone," I said. "I just found out that's he's in town. He's the only cat I know who has the kind of organization that could pull off an operation like this."

Bruno looked skeptical. "I've heard of him. Doesn't seem like his style. He got something against you in particular?"

I tossed my head in bewilderment. "There's the rub. He always liked me. Tried to recruit me, as a matter of fact. He knows his daughter and I—well, he knows his daughter has a thing for me."

"Lucky you," the dog said. "That could be it right there."

"What I don't understand is why he'd hire this Norwegian brute. The Don likes to keep things in the family."

"Well, nice knowing you, Stink," Bruno said.

I knew what he was getting at. Cats who crossed paws with Don Catleone had a habit of disappearing. Permanently.

"Yes," I said grimly. "Right, then. Let me know if you hear anything." I headed home.

When I returned to the house, Kitty was nowhere in sight.

Unbelievable. Her first day.

I looked closely at the cat door. My whisker was missing! No doubt Kitty had gone inside and was, at that very moment, eating my food.

But when I went into the house, I could find her nowhere on the first floor. I bounded upstairs to Aaron's bedroom. The ant carcasses had been vacuumed up, and the smell of ant spray lingered in the air. But I detected another smell—a cat!

"Hello, James," a voice said.

I spun around. Isabella was curled up in my bed.

"You!"

"Slumming, I see," she said. "I had expected you to

74

be staying at the Palace Hotel, at least. It took me longer to find you than I thought."

"You let the ants out, didn't you?" I said accusingly.

"James," she said, her voice tinged with hurt. "The ants were already out when I got here."

I stared at her for a long moment. "What do you want?"

Her expression became serious. "I told you. My father wants to talk to you."

"Is he behind all this?" I asked. "If he went after my boy—"

"Would I be here if he had?" she asked. Her face was sincere. "Please, James. Come and see him. For me. I promise it will be worth your while."

For all I knew, I was walking straight into a trap. But if the Don was going after my family and me, I needed to know why. Finally, I said with a flick of my tail, "Very well. Lead on."

I paused on the back porch and looked around. "By the way, what did you do with Kitty?"

Isabella pointed to a tangled web of garden hose, where a squirming Kitty was meowing piteously.

"You should really get a better secretary," Isabella said.

★ ★ ★

As we walked through the streets of Woodland Park, it almost seemed like old times.

"So," I said finally. "How long have you been in New Jersey?"

"Quite a while now. But my father still misses the old country."

"How is your brother?" I asked. Her younger brother was always getting into trouble. Took after the old man.

"Michael's made some enemies. He's spending the year in Sicily," Isabella said dryly.

"So is your father still grooming him to take over the business?" I asked with a laugh.

"Actually," she said, "my father's grooming *me* to take over."

"I see," I said dully.

"James," she said. "I'm sorry things can't be different."

"They can be," I said.

She twitched a whisker. "I—I—"

"Bella." I put my paw on hers.

She looked at me and then said, "We're here."

We were standing in front of Nino's Steaks and Chops, looking in the window.

Nino's obviously catered to an interesting crowd, for every man in the room was wearing a dark suit with a telltale bulge by the handkerchief pocket of his jacket.

"Keeping good company as always, I see," I said.

"This way," Isabella said.

She led me down an alley to an open side door, and into the kitchen. The scent of tomato and garlic and spicy sausage wafted enticingly through the air. There's nothing quite like the smell of an authentic Italian kitchen.

We continued down a red-painted hallway with a tin ceiling. At the end of the hallway, another door was open.

Sitting on a large leather couch was a prosperous-looking Bobtail cat with long, well-groomed hair. He looked older than I remembered, but just as imposing.

"Have a seat, James," the Don said in a husky voice. He waved a paw at an array of food in front of him. "Have some of the chicken liver pâté. The chef uses salmon oil. It's very good, James," he said and then grinned, displaying two razor-sharp, gold-tipped fangs. "Or should I call you Mr. Stink?"

I raised an eyebrow, but I didn't touch the food. "You have good information."

"Always, James," he said. "Speaking of information, I understand you have been having some trouble lately."

I gritted my teeth. "Nothing I can't handle. What do you want?"

"James, James, always leaping to the business. Have some food. It's truly exceptional. Food is what makes life worth living. Business is just how we get by," the Don said.

We stared at each other implacably.

The Don motioned with his head at a small dish of sparkling springwater, and I noticed that he had one in front of him, too. "At least let us have a toast to my daughter's health. *Salud!*" He leaned over to lap up the water.

I looked at Isabella, who gave me an encouraging nod, and I followed suit.

"There," the Don said, licking his lips. "Now we're friends. And friends keep an eye out for each other, do they not?"

"So do enemies," I said.

The Don laughed deeply. "I always liked you, James. You remind me of myself when I was your age. Always thinking you can take on the world all by yourself." In a flash, he grew sober. "Listen, I'm still involved in, shall we say, the import-export business. Food . . . catnip . . . you understand. So much more pleasant than diamonds, don't you agree?"

I snorted.

"Recently, someone has been trying to move in on my territory. I cleaned house, but the problem is not in my litter box. Whoever it is, he's smart. Extremely smart, and he knows how to cover his tracks. Sound familiar?"

"What are you trying to say?" I asked.

"Isn't it obvious? You and I have the same flea, and it needs to be . . . exterminated." He paused meaningfully. "Got any leads?"

"One or two," I said, giving him a hard look.

"James, I'm shocked by what you're suggesting. Shocked!" The Don did indeed look shocked. "You and I, we are cats of honor, are we not?" He was referring to the Feline Code of Honor, which all cats of breeding are obliged to follow. "Only a cat without honor would poison another cat's human. It's barbaric."

I clenched my jaw and took this in miserably. "Then I've run into another dead end." A refrigerator-size dead end.

The Don nodded. "Perhaps I can help you, my friend. You might be interested to know that there's been a lot of activity in the basement of the Happy Clown Ice Cream Stand on South Seventh Avenue, next to the hotel. I sent one of my best cats there to check it out. You remember my brother, Spike? Ahh, I see you do."

I caught myself rubbing my chin. I did indeed remember Bobby "Spike" Catleone. He was missing an eye, but he still fought like a crazed lion, as I had discovered during the diamond sting in Europe. I had a scar under my chin thanks to him.

"Spike hasn't come back," the Don said, his face grim.

I considered this and took another drink of water. "Then my enemy is even more dangerous than I had thought." I glanced at Bella, and then looked the Don square in the eye. "Do you know who he is?"

The Don threw his head back and laughed. "Come, come, James. Surely you're up for a little reconnaissance. A little Dumpster diving, perhaps?" He leaned forward. "How else will you know for sure that I'm telling you the truth?"

How else, indeed?

Dumpster diving was one of the least glamorous bits of tradecraft I had learned from the humans at

MI9, and yet it was one of the most useful tools in a spy's arsenal. You'd be surprised what people will throw away, all the while thinking their operations are perfectly secure. A chance scrap of paper, a candy wrapper, a discarded coffee cup: all these can yield a wealth of information to the trained eye.

Behind the Happy Clown, in a pile of garbage and buried under a half-eaten chicken carcass, I found what I was looking for: a packet of cat treats that some cat had torn into greedily, ripping it hastily open with his claws.

Except this cat was unusual: he had one claw too many.

The mastermind behind it all was a six-toed cat.

11

Baiting the Trap

MY WINDOW ledge in Aaron's room was an ideal spot to sort out my thoughts. The only six-toed cat I knew who had reason to hate me—and Sir Archibald—was Macavity, the arms dealer's fluffy white Persian. Part of me found it hard to believe he was truly behind all this: he was just a failed showcat.

Still, all the pieces did seem to fit. The poisoned biscuits. My rerouting to America. The threatening white whiskers. The remarkable pet food thefts. But why was he so bent on revenge? Putting away his human was part of our game, the spy business. Both sides knew the rules.

If Macavity was behind it all, as I now suspected, he was far smarter than I had assumed. He had already anticipated my every move, and I knew from personal experience that Spike Catleone was no slouch at cat burglary. A direct assault on the Happy Clown Ice Cream Stand was out of the question.

There had to be a weakness, I mused, staring out the window as rain fell on the darkened streets of Woodland Park. Aaron's bedroom was quiet save for the gunfire coming from the small television, and the occasional irritated smack as one of the boys killed a stray ant. Aaron and Robby were on the bed, playing a covert ops video game on his console. Personally, I found it a bit unrealistic: all they did was run around in a maze at top speed, shooting at each other. There was nothing covert about it.

Both boys were depressed after finding their science fair project destroyed. I vowed to make it up to the boys after I dealt with my own problem.

Suddenly, Aaron put down the controller. "I got it. We could do a maze," he said with a touch of excitement.

Robby blew away Aaron's on-screen spy before answering. "A maze? How is that science-y?"

"A maze that mice run through!"

"Hmmm. Maybe," Robby said in a dubious voice. "Where do we get the mice?"

"My dad's store," Aaron said, and then he frowned. "Actually, he doesn't carry mice, but he does have gerbils."

Robby shrugged. "Gerbils could work."

Aaron grinned.

"This could be cool," Robby said with a smile.

"Cooler than a stupid ant farm."

"Hey," Robby said. "So what do we use as bait? Gerbils don't eat cheese."

Bait! That was the answer to my problem!

Thanks to Frankie and Vinnie, by the following evening the entire town knew that Parkside Pet Foods had received a new shipment of Le Chat Gourmet.

Of course, there was no new shipment expected until next month. With the help of Isabella, I fished an empty bag of Le Chat Gourmet out of our trash at home and dragged it all the way to the store and in through the still-open skylight. We also brought along the yarn tail of the SuperMouse 99. On our way in, I snagged the tail on one of the highest shelves, with its little bell hanging down. Any animal entering the store through the skylight would jingle the bell, and my sensitive ears would pick it up instantly.

Inside, the store was dark and quiet. The piranhas stared at us balefully as we climbed down the shelves and made our way to the storeroom. The gerbils were asleep, and we took care not to wake them. We filled the empty bag most of the way with cheap bulk food that Mr. Green kept behind the counter for visiting strays.

And then I climbed inside.

"Are you sure you know what you're doing, James?" Isabella asked fearfully.

"I'm certain of it," I said in a firm voice.

"Be careful," she cried. She leaned forward to rub whiskers with me.

"I'll find your uncle," I promised as she nosed the bag shut.

Dead or alive.

Sometime after midnight, I woke to the sound of the bell tail jingling. (Yes, I must confess, I fell asleep in the bag.) Once. Twice. Thrice. Three cats had entered the store and were making their way down the aquarium racks from the skylight.

"Shhhh!" one of them said. "Don't wake dem gerbils."

"Aw, who gives a whiska," another snapped. "What they gonna do?"

"Both a yous, shut yer traps," said the third.

I peered out through a tiny hole in the bag as they came into the storeroom. All three were mangy strays. I recognized one of them—a regular that Mr. Green fed. Oh, the ingratitude. They were hardly the caliber of operatives I would have expected Macavity to rely upon, and for a moment I began to doubt my conclusions. They stopped in front of the alarm panel.

"Rats. They fixed the alarm."

"So bite it again!"

"I can't. They put metal pipe around the wires."

I smiled.

"We gotta keep moving. Never mind the alarm."

Quick as lightning, the cats converged on the shelf nearest the loading-dock door. They climbed up to the same level as the bar on the door and lined up.

"On three," one of them said. He was half bald with the mange. "One. Two. THREE!"

Simultaneously, they launched themselves at the door, striking the emergency panel at the same moment. The door burst outward, instantly setting off the alarm.

As the deafening bell began to ring, a steady stream of cats poured in, swarming among the shelves. Behind them strode the giant cat who had assaulted me at the hotel, looming hugely above them.

"You idiots! You forgot to disable te alarm."

"They're onto us, Sven," the balding cat whined. "There was metal pipe around the wires."

Sven. It was a name as Norwegian as his accent. Now I knew why his voice sounded so familiar. He was one of the cats who had been speaking when I was drugged and in my cat carrier at the airport. He was responsible for me being sent to America!

Sven whirled in anger and shouted in his deep,

accented voice. "Sixty seconds. Move, ja? Or I make you into violins!" He held the door propped open as a few stragglers streamed in.

"Here! I found it!" shrieked a black cat. He was so thin, his eyes seemed to pop out of his head. "There's only one bag, but it's already open!"

"Take anyting you can find."

Immediately, the cats swarmed around the bag I was in, some taking a corner in their mouth, another holding the opening closed with his teeth. Together, they dragged the bag off the bottom shelf and toward the loading dock.

"Ten seconds," I heard Sven shout.

I tumbled end-over-end inside the bag as they dragged me down the steps.

And then I lost consciousness.

When I came to, everything was dark and smelled of cat food. A good sign: I was still inside the bag. I listened carefully. I heard the murmur of a number of cats talking, but none of them seemed on their guard. I was safe. I lifted the open corner of the bag and peered out.

I was on top of an enormous pile of cat food bags of numerous different brands in what was apparently the basement of the Happy Clown. Beyond, I could see row upon row of street cats—spindly, malnourished, and exhausted-looking. At first glance, they appeared to be batting bits of dry food about with their paws, but then I realized their game. They were sorting cat food, cutting cheap cat food with expensive premium cat food.

A small number of heavily muscled cats paced back and forth behind them, urging them to work faster. I spotted one small kitten sneak a mouthful of the food he was sorting, only to be stunned by a blow from the heavy paw of one of the guards.

"This food isn't for you," the guard snarled. "It's for the customers."

"But I'm *so hungry*," the kitten whined.

"Watch it or *you'll* end up in the food. Get back to work."

I needed a way to get closer, to blend in. Unfortunately, I was in perfect health, recently brushed by Aaron, in fact. I would never be able to pass for a spindly, underfed street cat. I glanced around, looking for something I could use to fashion a disguise.

Then I saw it. In a corner of the basement, a leaky steam pipe had created a puddle of watery mud. With my fur wet and matted down, I knew I would make a fairly convincing street cat. I had seen myself once when Sir Archibald had been compelled to give me a bath to rinse off a potentially toxic compound I had been exposed to on one of our missions. I had resembled nothing so much as a bedraggled rat with bat ears.

Keeping the heap of food bags between myself and the rest of the room, I rolled around in the slurry until I was fully disguised. A skinny, brown, filthy urchin. I made a rather good street cat, if I did say so myself. And then I heard a voice behind me.

"Vell, vell, vell," the cat growled menacingly.

I whirled around and there he was. . . .

Sven.

12

I Die a Horrible Death

YOU AGAIN," the Norwegian beast said, flexing his razor-sharp claws.

One of the few breeds larger, on average, than the Bengal is the formidable Norwegian Forest Cat, and Sven was a prime specimen.

"Perhaps we can discuss this like gentlecats," I ventured, slowly backing toward the wall. I knew my blunt claws were completely useless in this situation. Oh, for a scratching post! My litter box for a scratching post!

"No discussion," Sven said in his deep basso. "Ve can do dis t' hard vay or t' easy vay, Mr. Stinki."

"Well," I said, stalling for time as I continued to back

up, "I have always been a fan of the *hard way*."

At this, I lashed out with everything I had, catching Sven across the face with what would have been a knockout blow to any normal cat, even with my claws in their poor condition.

Sven barely grunted. "Okay. Ve do it t' hard vay." He advanced on me like a freight train, grinning broadly.

Here was a cat who enjoyed his work. Whatever Sven had in the bulk department, however, he clearly lacked in the brain department.

I continued to back up until my hindquarters touched the enormous mountain of food bags.

"Novere to run, Stinki," he chortled, towering over me. "Now you can say good-bye to yer smelly little tail, ja?"

"Who said anything about running, my friend?" I said.

Sven cracked his knuckles and lashed out at me, claws gleaming in the dim light.

I ducked, leaping out of the way. Sven's blow landed on one of the bags, ripping a wide gash and releasing a landslide of food. Unbalanced, Sven stumbled, fell forward, and was immediately buried up to his torn ear in food. Karmic Kitty, if I wasn't mistaken.

"And for the record, Sven," I said, "I don't smell."

★ ★ ★

Keeping to the edges of the basement, I avoided being noticed by any other guards and soon found myself in a hallway of refrigerated storerooms marked ICE CREAM CAKES, ICE CREAM SANDWICHES, and so on, including one devoted to ROCKY ROAD, evidently a popular flavor.

Then I heard a tapping from behind a door marked POPSICLES. With a great leap, I managed to smack the handle of the door, which bounced open to reveal—

A frozen Spike. Or, I should say, a Spikecicle.

Spike was a sorry sight. Ice was crusted in his fur, and he was shivering so hard, he looked like a windup toy.

He blinked, his features showing surprise as he recognized me. "I suppose my n-n-n-niece sent you. Thanks. Another f-f-f-few minutes and I would have been a g-g-g-goner."

I helped him to his feet. "Actually, your brother sent me. It's a long story. Let's get you out of here."

"No," he croaked. "I c-c-c-ame here to do a job and I'll do it. I gotta take out the cat upstairs. A b-b-b-big Persian."

A Persian!

"Does he . . . by any chance . . . have six toes?"

Spike's brow furrowed, and ice cracked off his whiskers. "You know him?"

"Let's go," I said grimly.

Spike led us through a confusing set of tunnels and up a set of back stairs to a door.

"That's his office," Spike whispered. "You kick open the door and I'll rush him."

I didn't think Spike was in any shape to rush anybody, so I said, "Why don't we just see if he's in there
first?"

Spike nodded, and I quietly pushed the door open,
peering inside.

It was a nondescript office, except for the little fact
that there was a full-scale map of Woodland Park on
the wall. Circled in red were the Palace Hotel, the
Happy Clown, Nino's, and . . . #9 North Tenth
Avenue!

I heard a bone-chilling laugh that made the fur on
my tail stand on end. It was the laugh of ultimate
evil.

A white Persian cat emerged from the center of a
group of henchcats. He was holding—yes, *holding*—
a small pawful of cat treats. His extra toes were set at
an angle and served as opposable thumbs. His head
swiveled slowly from side to side, reminding me of a
snake.

Spike was right behind me. "Time for you to pack
up your litter box and go back wherever you came
from. This is Catleone family territory, see?"

But Macavity ignored Spike and locked eyes with
me.

I had been hardly more than a kitten when I faced

him before. My last memory of him was hearing the same laugh in the darkness belowdecks of the arms dealer's yacht, off the coast of Monte Carlo.

"You haven't seen the last of me," he'd cackled.

It seems he was right.

"Let me handle this, Spike," I growled, staring at Macavity.

I felt a flicker of fear. Here, at last, I was face-to-face with the cat who had killed my Sir Archibald.

"I've been expecting you, Mr. Stink," he purred. "Or should I say . . . Bristlefur?"

"You rogue," I growled. "You killed Sir Archibald."

"Oh, your suffering has just begun," he taunted me. He popped a cat treat into his mouth and chewed with relish. "By the way, how is your boy? Shame about his little experiment. But then, I've always been partial to dissections myself."

"You'll have nothing to do with my boy," I hissed, and puffed out my fur menacingly, preparing to strike. "Your nine lives are over!"

The six-toed cat gazed at me with infinite sadness. "I thought you were a worthy opponent, James, but now I see you are just like all the rest of them. Pity."

He turned tail and ran out the open door.

"Get him!" Spike shouted. "I can handle the others."

Extending his claws and baring his fangs, Spike flung himself at the henchcats, and I took off after Macavity.

"Raid! Raid!" a skinny cat cried, and chaos ensued.

I found myself back in the basement workroom dashing after Macavity as street cats ran in all directions, scrambling to get out. He ran through the middle of the room, knocking food over into the aisles, his long white fur flowing behind him. I followed him around a corner and up another set of dark stairs. Up, up, up, hot on his tail.

When I reached the top, I emerged onto the roof of the Happy Clown. Standing on the edge of the roof was Macavity. I watched with astonishment as he leaped across the expanse between the Happy Clown and the back roof of the Palace Hotel. Would he survive the leap?

He did, with barely a wobble, then turned to look at me.

"I always land on my feet, Bristlefur!" he shouted, and ran off.

I backed up, took a running leap, and found myself flying between the two buildings, the air brushing through my fur. My paws hit the roof with a sure thump. Far ahead of me, I saw Macavity's white tail disappear into an open door on the rooftop.

The top-floor hallways of the Palace Hotel were quiet. No doubt everyone was downstairs at the cat show.

There was a noise above me. I cocked an ear—and heard the distinct sound of paws clicking on metal.

He was in the ducts!

I ran over to a little hatch like the one Isabella had shown me and slipped into the dark depths of the hotel's ventilation system.

13

Cat Chowder

AND THAT is how Macavity led me on a chase through the ducts and straight into a trap. There I was, falling down a ventilation shaft toward the deadly blades of a whirling fan and certain doom. I flung out my paws to slow my descent.

I looked up, muscles trembling from the effort. The six-toed cat stared down from far above, an evil gleam in his eye.

"Do you expect me to beg for my life?" I asked with more bravado than I felt, scrabbling to gain purchase on the slick walls.

"No, Mr. Stink," he purred silkily. "I expect you to die."

There was a noise above, and Macavity glanced up.

"Pity I can't stand around and chat. See you in your next life," he cackled, and then he disappeared deeper into the ductwork.

I felt myself slip another foot. The sharp blades whirred, sending a brisk wind in my direction. I was only a whisker away from becoming cat pâté. *Le Stink Gourmet*, I thought.

"James!" Isabella shouted from above. "Hang on a little longer. I'll save you!"

"Bella!"

"Hold on. I'll find something you can sink your claws into, and Spike and I will drag you up." Spike's head appeared beside hers at the top of the shaft.

"No . . . time," I panted as I strained to hold myself steady. "Go after Macavity. Don't let him get away!"

"I won't leave you, James!"

"Do as I say!"

My legs gave out and I slipped.

It's all over, I thought, as I fell toward my certain death.

So this was how it was going to end for James Edward Bristlefur. I had always imagined something more heroic, like going over a cliff in a car chase, or maybe plunging over a waterfall locked in a death grip with a villain. But to fall into a fan and be chopped to pieces like yesterday's liver?

Ah well.

Below me, I heard a human say, "Hey, who left this fan on?"

Abruptly, the fan was shut off, and instead of falling into the blades, I slipped between them and crashed through a wire screen covering the opening below.

I still have the old Bristlefur luck! I thought.

That is, until I tumbled face first into a huge vat with a tremendous splash.

I came up sputtering. The warm liquid in the vat was thick and creamy and vaguely fishy-smelling. I licked my whiskers. Clam chowder.

How undignified.

Not even bothering to give myself a bath, I dashed out the rear door of the kitchen and into a back alleyway, tracking chowder everywhere.

The basement of the Happy Clown had been completely cleaned out. It was as if no one had ever been there.

Someone stumbled behind me, and I whirled around, paws raised.

It was Spike, battered and bleeding. One of his ears had a fresh notch in it. I caught the anguish in his one eye, and my heart stilled.

"They got Isabella."

Spike would not let me accompany him to Nino's Steaks and Chops to tell Don Catleone what had happened to his daughter.

"This is a matter for the family now," he said in a tight voice. "Go home."

I wasn't about to give up. I would check in with the Greens and regroup. Then I would set out and find Isabella.

Needless to say, my humans were not at all pleased to see me when I arrived at dinnertime covered in caked mud and dried clam chowder. I stood placidly in the backyard while Mrs. Green hosed me off.

"You stink, Mr. Stink. What have you been up to all day?"

If she only knew.

She bundled me into a towel and brought me inside, where Mr. Green was full of news of the cat show.

"You're a lifesaver, sweetie. Thanks for remembering

that we had that bag of Le Chat Gourmet here. I had just enough samples to give out. I'd say over half the breeders at the show put in orders!"

"That's wonderful! Who won the show, anyway?"

"It was a real surprise," Mr. Green said. "I thought for sure this white Persian would win. He looked like a real pro, but he got disqualified when they discovered he had six toes. I thought he was going to scratch the judge's eyes out."

Upstairs, the talk was of animals of another sort.

Sitting in the middle of the bedroom floor was an elaborate maze built out of plywood. I must say I was impressed with the boys' ingenuity—the maze walls were fitted onto pegs and could be moved, resulting in a large number of possible maze configurations. Both boys were holding clipboards and stopwatches. Apparently, they were timing the gerbils' progress through the maze to see if they were learning how to do it faster over time.

"Ow!" Aaron yelped as one of the gerbils nipped his finger. I noticed that he was wearing several bandages on his other fingers.

"Where did your dad get these gerbils anyway?" Robby asked in frustration. He was holding a pencil and was poking at one of the gerbils gingerly, but the gerbil absolutely refused to move either forward or backward.

"The Island of Evil Animals, I think," Aaron said with a sigh. "I wouldn't mind being bitten if they weren't so stupid."

I heard the distinct sound of the gerbil chomping down on the end of the pencil. *You're the stupid one! You keep putting your fingers near us!*

I advanced on the gerbil with a growl, and Aaron leaped in front of me.

"No, Mr. Stink. These are for a science project. You can't eat them."

Pity, I purred to the gerbils, who had ceased their laughing. *Bite my boy again and, rest assured, it shall be the last bite you ever take.*

The gerbil stared at me defiantly.

"Stan McCann told me he was doing a robot that can follow a line on the floor," Robby said in a miserable voice.

Aaron stared hard at the gerbils, and a look of resolve entered his eye. "We've got one more day to work on it. We're not giving up. Got it?"

Robby nodded.

"I have an idea," Aaron said, and dashed out of the

room, only to return a moment later holding a pair of oven mitts. "Protection."

That's my boy, I thought. Patience and persistence. He might make a good spy one day.

Aaron took a deep breath and slipped on the mitts. "Okay, let's try the other gerbil."

I stayed out all night and into the next morning, scouring Woodland Park, looking for any sign of Isabella or Macavity. But no one had seen a trace of either of them.

"A pterodactyl?" Frankie squeaked. "I thought dinosaurs was extinct?"

"Polydactyl," I snapped. "A cat with six toes."

Vinnie screwed his face up. "You mean like dey got a thumb or something?"

"Exactly."

"Are you pulling my tail? Oh wait, I don't got a tail," Frankie griped.

"We'll keep an eye out for your girlfriend," Vinnie said reassuringly.

"She's just a friend," I said. "A very good friend."

The two mice winked at each other.

As I walked down the block, a feeling of despair washed over me. It was all my fault that Macavity had Isabella. I had forgotten Sir Archibald's first rule of thumb: never underestimate the opposition. Because of my failure in this regard, Isabella would soon share Sir Archibald's fate. I had to find her, and fast. But they could be miles away by now.

A dog barked in the distance. *That's it!* I thought. *The Bark Network!*

I ran over to Bruno's house and explained the situation to him. He nodded and immediately began to bark. I could hear the faint sound of dogs barking in reply from as far away as several miles, but it sounded like gibberish.

"Why can't I understand what they're saying?" I asked.

"It's encrypted," he said, and held up a paw for patience, ears cocked. "I'm getting in reports now."

A golden retriever from the next block started barking loudly, relaying the news. From the expression on Bruno's face, it didn't look good.

Bruno shook his head. "Sorry, Stink. No sign of her from here to Atlantic City."

This was maddening! An organization of the size I had seen operating out of the Happy Clown could not simply vanish into thin air.

"Keep trying," I said. "Macavity would take her to the last place we would expect."

Suddenly, Bruno began to growl menacingly. I turned to see Kitty running toward us.

"What do *you* want, ya little thief?" Bruno asked.

Kitty skidded to a stop mere steps from me, but well out of range of Bruno.

"I'm no thief! I've gone legit," she said, panting and out of breath.

I gestured for her to ignore him. "What is it, Kitty?"

"A cat came by the house with a message for you," she said in a rush.

"So what's the message?" Bruno growled.

She squinted, trying to remember the exact words. "He said to tell you that Macavity wants to see you. And you're supposed to come alone, or else."

Standard stuff. I made an impatient noise. "Yes, yes, where do I meet him?"

Kitty wiggled her nose. "He didn't say. All he said was, 'Check your dead drop,' whatever that is. Does that mean anything to you?"

I narrowed my eyes. How did Macavity know about my dead drop? Unless . . . I was filled with an ominous foreboding. I whirled and ran off.

"Stink, wait! Let me call you some backup!" Bruno barked.

"No time!" I called back.

I raced to Parkside Pet Foods.

Out back behind the Dumpster was the dead drop I had told the wharf rat about. It was an old wooden cigar box. I easily flipped open the hinged lid with my paw. Lying inside was the body of the wharf rat, dead.

No, wait, merely unconscious. And he had been . . . shaved?

Frankie and Vinnie were just strolling up to the loading dock to deliver their daily report, and they came over to see what I was doing.

"Who's dat?" Vinnie asked.

"My informant."

"I thought *we* was your informants," Vinnie whined.

"He don't look so good." Frankie fingered the stub of his tail. "You're a dangerous cat to work for, Mr. Stink."

I prodded the wharf rat firmly with one paw, and he blinked an eye open, groaning. "What happened?"

Vinnie was still looking at the wharf rat, his eyes wide. "How come ya don't give *us* jewels?"

Jewels?

Then I noticed. The rat had Isabella's diamond necklace around his neck!

14

Weird Science

AFTER DEBRIEFING the rat, I left him in Frankie and Vinnie's care and went around to the front of the store. The door was open, and when I walked in, "How Much Is That Doggy . . ." immediately started playing. I meowed at the device irritably.

Mr. Green looked up from the counter, where he was standing and reading a copy of *Cat Fancy*. He seemed in bright spirits, which only served to worsen my mood.

"Where've you been all day, Mr. Stink? Out mousing?" he asked, picking up a large box from the cat show.

"Look what I got you," he said.

Then he pulled out of the box the most amazing-looking scratching post I had ever seen. It was a tall, freestanding post with cardboard on one side, carpet on another, rope on a third, and wood on a fourth.

"Pretty cool, huh? It's the Scratch-X 4000. I picked it up at the cat show. Some Finnish company invented it," Mr. Green said, pleased at my reaction. "Try it out."

The timing could not have been more perfect. I would need my claws in fighting trim for the upcoming confrontation with Macavity. As my claws shredded the cardboard, I went over my conversation with the rat.

"Next thing I knew, here I am," the rat said. "Oy! They must've ambushed me tail."

"Why did he shave you?" I asked.

"Shave?" The rat looked down and squeaked in dismay. "Crikey! My belly! I'm bald as the vicar's old cat!"

I was certain that it was a clue as to where Isabella was being held. Macavity was testing me. But what did it mean?

That night Aaron and Robby put the gerbils through their paces for a final time, while I looked on. The gerbils kept glancing at me fearfully. They had wisely taken my advice and were cooperating.

"He did it in under a minute!" Aaron exclaimed, looking at his stopwatch. He looked at me curiously. "Do you think Mr. Stink is scaring them into running faster?"

"Whatever it is, we are so going to win," Robby said, putting a cap on his head. "I'll meet you back here in the morning to help pack everything up. What time?"

"Eight," Aaron said. "Mom will drive us over in the minivan."

"Your dad coming?"

"Uh, sure," Aaron said, sounding not at all sure.

After Robby left, I curled up on my cat bed, and Aaron brushed me.

"Good job, Mr. Stink. If we win tomorrow, you'll get cat treats all week!" Aaron promised.

The combination of the soothing brush and the exertion of the last few days was too much. I fell asleep immediately.

I was back in London, running through the halls of MI9 headquarters. How I missed it. The lobby with its fine blue carpet like mole fur, and the wooden emblem hanging above the reception desk with its Latin motto: Omnino Fictum.

But there were no people. The building was deserted. I looked everywhere—the briefing room, the orbital-monitoring station, the shooting range, the cafeteria—all to no avail.

Then I rounded the corner and saw the MI9 science lab with its gleaming stainless steel tables. Science lab? Suddenly,

Macavity's words rang in my ears:

"But then, I've always been partial to dissections myself."

I awoke with a start.

The rat's belly wasn't shaved for surgery—it was shaved for . . . dissection!

Macavity was keeping Isabella at the school in the science lab! Right under my whiskers the whole time! I was so happy I could have hugged my boy. But when I looked over at him, there was a terrible expression on his face.

"What have you done?" Aaron exploded.

He pointed at the gerbil cage. It was empty!

"Mom!" Aaron shouted. "Mr. Stink ate the gerbils!"

It wasn't me! I wanted to shout back. Macavity again! Drat the foul beast!

Mrs. Green rushed upstairs. "Oh no, honey, he didn't, did he?"

Aaron looked stricken. "They're gone! I know I locked the cage last night."

Robby walked into the room, backpack slung over one shoulder. "Ready to go?" His eyes went to the cage. "Hey—where are the gerbils?"

There was a moment of silence as all eyes turned to me.

"Oh, no," Robby said.

"What are we gonna do?" Aaron asked, panic in his voice. "They'll never believe it if we say the cat ate our homework. It's the oldest line in the book!"

"Can't you call your dad at the store and ask him to bring some new gerbils?" Robby asked.

"Those were the only ones in the cage," Aaron said.

Mrs. Green stared at me. "Well, then we'll take Mr. Stink and show him to the judges ourselves! They'll believe you then."

She grabbed me by the scruff of the neck and carried me to the garage while the boys packed up. As we drove down the driveway, I shouted a message to Kitty out the open window of the minivan.

And hurry! I urged. *There is no time to lose!*

Aaron wouldn't even look at me on the ride over. The minivan pulled in to a spot in the crowded school parking lot. The boys hopped out and began to lift the maze out of the back of the minivan. The door was open. I didn't hesitate—I dashed out of the minivan and across the parking lot.

"Come back here, Mr. Stink!" Mrs. Green shouted.

They would have to wait. I had a lady to rescue.

I followed my nose down the hallways to the science lab, passing the large auditorium, where kids were setting up their science projects for the fair. A sign over the door read COUNTY SCIENCE FAIR.

Creeping carefully along, I soon picked up Macavity's telltale scent. It led right to the door of a lab classroom, just as I had suspected. I pushed the door open and entered.

The lights were off. But I could see perfectly; I had excellent night vision. The room contained several rows of lab benches with black stone countertops, each with a sink and a nozzle for a Bunsen burner. High stools were lined up at each bench. I jumped up onto the nearest one.

"I hope you came alone," Macavity's voice came out of the darkness. "I wouldn't want anything to *happen* to the lovely Isabella here."

A light suddenly flicked on to reveal Isabella duct-taped into a large dissection tray in front of me. Her mouth was taped shut, but I could see the fear in her eyes. Next to her in the sink was a rubber bucket of dry ice, no doubt part of some experiment down the hall.

I looked in the direction of the light and saw Macavity perched above us on one of the shelving units that lined the walls. He had turned on a desk lamp that was sitting next to him, and the glare blinded me slightly.

"Very 'handy,' the extra toe." He smiled and wiggled a paw at me.

"Let her go and take me instead," I said.

"But that would spoil the fun!" he said with a cackle, high above us.

I made a move to jump onto the shelf, but he shook his head.

"I wouldn't take another step if I were you." He moved and glassware clinked. He was surrounded by delicate instruments and beakers. The one right next to him was steaming. "Hydrochloric acid. Interesting what you can find in a fifth-grade science lab. I'd hate there to be some kind of . . . *accident*."

I growled and flexed my claws. "Come down here and I'll—"

"You'll what?" Macavity laughed throatily. "Always trying to use brute force rather than brains, Bristlefur. When are you going to learn?"

"Why are you doing this?"

"Why?" he snarled. "Are you really that stupid? You ruined my life!"

"Oh, come *on*," I snorted. "Your human knew the rules of the game."

"So it's a *game* to you? My human died in that prison." Macavity read the surprise on my face and stomped in fury. "You didn't even know he was dead!"

I hadn't known. Still, I didn't much care. "He was selling nuclear weapons to the highest bidder!"

"He was good to me!"

"Regardless, I've put you out of business. You might as well give up gracefully."

He laughed again. "You think the basement of the Happy Clown was my only operation? Your feeble mind cannot even comprehend how far my web extends. But no matter." He waved a paw. "Before you, you will notice a bowl of cream. Just like the cream you were meant to drink the night I poisoned Sir Archibald."

I remembered the bowl of cream.

"I wanted to get both of you, but somehow you slipped away," Macavity was saying. "I intend to correct that mistake."

"I didn't think geniuses made mistakes." I looked at the sink, a plan forming in my mind. But I was stalling, and Macavity knew it.

His expression hardened. "Now, drink the cream, James, and I might let your girlfriend live. Who knows, maybe she'll come and work for me."

I stared at Isabella. Her eyes were begging me to do no such thing.

"Drink the cream!" Macavity snarled.

I bent my head toward the bowl, and then leaped for the hot water tap of the sink, knocking hard against it. A jet of water struck the dry ice in the bucket, and a thick fog exploded upward. It spread out across the lab bench, spilling over the sides and obscuring Macavity's view from above. I dashed over to the dissection tray and pushed it onto the floor. Isabella might get a few bruises, but I had barely enough time.

CRASH!

A beaker smashed into the lab bench where I had been standing a moment before, shards of glass raining on me. It was close, too close.

Sir Archibald's words of advice to MI9 recruits came to me in that moment.

"Spying is our game," he liked to say. "Never let an opponent dictate the play."

I had been letting Macavity make the rules for long enough. It was time to take control of the game. And I knew just what button to push.

"So tell me," I taunted him deliberately. "What's it like to show in the Household Pet Category? The competition from the goldfish must be formidable."

I heard Macavity's growl of outrage a moment before all twelve pounds of Macavity landed on top of me. His face was so close to mine that I could smell Le Chat Gourmet on his breath.

"Time to wipe that smile off your face," Macavity snarled, raising a paw to strike.

"I think not," I said.

He lashed out, but I had spent many hours watching MI9 operatives train for just such a situation. I twisted, dodging his blow, then sprang, catching him square across the face with my razor-sharp claws. He yowled in pain as four bright red gashes appeared across one side of his face.

"Guess you'll never be Best in Show," I said, tensing for another blow.

The door to the classroom slammed against the wall. I turned to see an army of grim-faced cats pouring into the room, with Spike in the lead. The Catleone family had arrived! I spun back around to see Macavity leaping to the next lab bench.

"You haven't seen the last of me, Bristlefur!" Macavity cried. He leaped to the venetian blinds and slipped through an open window.

He was gone.

15

Le Chat Gourmet

SPIKE GLARED at me as he and several Catleones freed his niece from the duct tape.

"Ouch," Isabella said, arching her back in a stretch. "That was some rescue."

"Thanks," I said. "I think."

She winked at me. "We can talk later. Your boy needs you."

"Indeed."

Back in the gymnasium, Aaron and Robby were standing in front of their project—"Those A-MAZE-ing Gerbils!"—and were waiting anxiously for the judges, who had just come into view at the end of their row. I walked up to the chair where Mrs. Green was sitting and jumped up onto her lap. I was exhausted.

"Kind of you to drop by, seeing as how this is all your fault," she said irritably. "You're skating on thin ice with me, cat. You destroyed our couch. We've got ants in the house. Who knows where those gerbils are! You'd better watch out or you're going back to the Humane Society."

I purred to show her that everything would work out fine.

"Hmph. Nice try," she said. But I could tell she was softening.

The judges drew nearer and were making appreciative noises in front of Stan McCann's robot project. They looked at each other, nodding, and made some notes on their clipboards.

"So what are we going to say?" Robby was asking.

Aaron's mouth was a thin, grim line. "We'll tell them what happened. It's the truth. Mom will back us up."

Robby didn't look convinced. "They won't care. The fact is—"

Suddenly, the double doors to the parking lot opened and Mr. Green burst in. His tie was loose and he was sweating. "I made it!" He was carrying a small cage in one hand, and he made a beeline for the boys. He showed them the cage. "I didn't remember ordering these, but there they were in the gerbil cage."

"Those aren't gerbils!" Robby said. "They're mice!"

Frankie and Vinnie were sitting nervously in the cage. Clearly, they had gotten my message from Kitty.

"It's okay," Aaron said. He grabbed an extra piece of construction paper and started cutting out an *M*. "They'll be good enough."

I prayed they would.

By the time the judges arrived in front of "Those A-MAZE-ing MICE," I was sitting on the table, briefing the mice in their cage.

"Now listen closely. The configuration of the maze is left, left, right, right, left, right, left."

Vinnie wrinkled his nose in concentration. "Gotcha. Left, left, right, right—"

"Which one is left again?" Frankie interrupted, looking at his paws.

I sighed. "Vinnie, you run the maze."

And then there was no more time. "'Those A-MAZE-ing Mice.' Good title," one of the judges said, making a note. "So tell me about your project."

Robby spoke up. "We ran gerb— *mice* through a maze and timed them to see if they got faster with practice."

The other judge was looking at me. "What's with the cat?"

Robby shot me a sour look, but something about the gleam in Aaron's eye let me know that my boy hadn't given up completely on me.

"See, we wanted to be scientific and reproduce the exact conditions we had at home," Aaron explained. "Mr. Stink here was always watching us work, so we thought we'd have the best results if we brought him here, too."

The judge frowned. "That's rather unusual, but it is in keeping with the scientific principles of maintaining a consistent environment when running experiments." He looked at the graphs on the backdrop, which showed how quickly the gerbils had run through the maze. "Those are some impressive times. *If* these results are real. Let's see 'em."

Aaron and Robby looked at each other and gulped.

This was Vinnie's big moment. Robby reached into the cage and pulled out . . .

Frankie.

Oh no, I groaned.

I can do it, boss, Frankie said as Robby set him down at one end of the maze.

Aaron placed me next to the cage and whispered, "Get those mice moving, Mr. Stink!"

Robby clicked his stopwatch.

Go, go! I meowed, and Frankie took off. *Left! No, the other left!*

Now Vinnie was squeaking too. *No, you dope. Left, left, right, right, left . . .*

Miraculously, Frankie made it through the maze and pounced on the food at the other end. Aaron clicked off his stopwatch.

"That's a record," Aaron said, pointing at the graphs. "You see," he went on, "we think the gerb— *mice* are so smart because the cat acts as a negative motivating factor, while at the same time the food acts as a positive one."

"Good one," Robby said quietly.

The two judges' eyebrows seemed to be glued to the tops of their heads. "Very, very impressive," one of them said at last.

"Yes, I've seen a lot of mouse mazes in these science fairs over the years," the other judge said. "But I've never seen a mouse run that fast."

I was hungry! Frankie squeaked, his mouth full. *I*

didn't have breakfast dis morning.

My boy patted me on the head. It was all the thanks I needed.

The boys won second place in the science fair.

"All right," Aaron said. "Second place!"

"Yeah," Robby said. "I bet we could have won first but, hey, let's face it, Stan McCann's robot *was* really cool."

Aaron turned to his father. "Thanks, Dad. You really came through for me."

Mr. Green hugged his son.

I heard the sound of purring behind me. It was Isabella, freed from the duct tape.

"Do you know where Macavity went?" she asked.

"No, but he'll be back. Of that you can be certain." I knew I would have to be on my guard from now on, if I wanted to protect the ones I loved. I cocked my head. "How did your father know we were at the school?"

Isabella laughed. "The gerbils."

"Gerbils?"

"They're my spies. That's how I knew you were in Woodland Park. When they escaped, they went straight to Nino's and told my father, which is how

Spike knew where I was being held."

"What do you mean, 'they escaped'?!"

"Yes, didn't you know? Your boy left the cage door open by mistake, and they were sick of the whole assignment." She shrugged. "I've already gotten replacements."

So that, at least, had not been Macavity.

"Maybe we can have dinner at Nino's sometime?" I asked.

She pursed her mouth. "We'll see. After all, I have a crime syndicate to run."

I nodded. She turned to leave.

"Bella?" I called.

"Yes?" she said.

"Never mind." And I let her go.

The next morning, when I went down to breakfast, Mr. Green was excitedly opening an envelope.

"It's from Le Chat Gourmet! Everybody be quiet," he said. He unfolded the letter and held it up.

Lily piped up. "Doesn't anybody want to hear how my gymnastics practice went yesterday?"

"No, Lily," Mr. Green and Aaron said simultaneously. Mr. Green began to read the letter out loud:

Dear Monsieur Green,

   Thank you for your recent entry into the "Who is Le Chat Gourmet?" Contest. Unfortunately, we did not like your essay very much. . . .

His face fell, and he scanned the page silently. Then he brightened, and continued to read aloud:

   Nevertheless, when we saw the photo of your cat, we knew in an instant that we had found the next Le Chat Gourmet. You have an exceptionally handsome cat, if we may say so.
   We are pleased to inform you that you have won the contest. You and your family will be treated to an all-expense-paid tour of France and a photo shoot in Paris with one of the world's top pet photographers. Congratulations, and keep feeding Monsieur Stink Le Chat Gourmet!

"We won! We won!" Mr. Green shouted.
We were going to France!

Authors' Addendum

OUR TRANSLATION efforts on the large collection of documents found in James Edward Bristlefur's safe house are proceeding on schedule. However, our task is greatly complicated by the disappearance of the true author, "Mr. Stink," as his closest friends knew him. We are told that he would often vanish mysteriously for long periods of time, but never for so long as in the current instance. We will forward any reliable information about his current whereabouts with the utmost priority.

We would like to recommend commendations to the following informants who have provided invaluable intelligence: C. Hutton, J. Grinberg, S. Moore. And for his nightly briefings, Will Aaron. Of course, all names have been changed to maintain their cover.

As before, we have tried to assemble Mr. Stink's

notes as accurately as possible. Any errors or omissions in the file are certainly our fault and not his.

Respectfully submitted,
Holm & Hamel
Special to MI9

Attention All Agents:
Have you seen Mr. Stink in your neighborhood?
Please report all sightings to findstink@stinkfiles.com.

THE TAIL ENDS HERE FOR NOW!

TURN THE PAGE FOR

A SNEAK PREVIEW OF . . .

Dossier 003:

YOU ONLY HAVE
NINE LIVES

THE WATER was up to my chin.

It was icy cold, and I knew I wouldn't last long, even if I could keep my head above it. To make things worse, the level was steadily rising.

Within moments, I was unable to touch the bottom with my feet. I began to paddle frantically with my paws, but the cold had worked its way into my muscles, and I was tiring fast. Every few seconds, my nose ducked beneath the water, and I came up sputtering.

In short, I was drowning like a rat.

"Enjoying your swim?" a voice called mockingly.

I looked up to see a cat grinning down over the edge of the deep shaft where he had trapped me. The stone walls were slick with moss, and there was no way to climb up. Sir Archibald had always advised his operatives to swim with the tide, but this was taking it a bit far, I thought.

"The water's lovely," I said, gasping for breath. "Why don't you come down and join me?"

"Oh, I don't think so," he cackled. "But I'm going to miss your sense of humor."

Water rushed into my mouth and I choked.

And to think I was supposed to be on holiday!

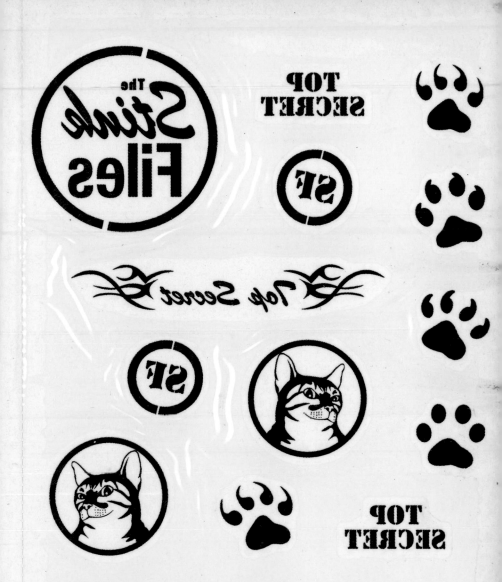

Hold the coded message up to a mirror to learn the title of Mr. Stink's next fur-raising adventure:

YOU ONLY HAVE NINE LIVES

HarperCollins*Publishers*   www.harperchildrens.com   www.stinkfiles.com

Ask an adult to help you!

Removable Tattoo Directions:
1. Cut out tattoo.
2. Peel off protective layer from the tattoo sheet.
3. Put tattoo facedown against skin, press firmly.
4. Wet back of tattoo with damp cloth or sponge.
5. Wait 30 seconds, slide paper backing off, and wipe lightly with a wet towel.

To remove, wipe gently with alcohol or baby oil.

NOTE: Do not apply to sensitive skin or near eyes.

Safe and nontoxic.

Ingredients: Acrylates/VA Copolymer; Castor Oil; Ethyl Cellulose; TC0011 Black.

Safety Tested and Non-Toxic